BLUEPRINT FOR LOVE

Hazel Dobson is pleased when she gets temp work at Gough Associates, an architectural company based in a beautiful manor house in Norfolk. While it's a far cry from the bright lights of London, she is keen to get away from a mundane job with a lecherous boss, and to spend some time with her great-aunt. There she meets handsome and wealthy Jonathan Gough, and sees a chance at happiness and a family with him. But some people just don't want Hazel and Jonathan to be happy . . .

HENRIETTE GYLAND

BLUEPRINT FOR LOVE

Complete and Unabridged

LINFORD
Leicester

First published in Great Britain in 2013
Choc Lit Limited
Surrey

First Linford Edition
published 2018
by arrangement with
Choc Lit Limited
Surrey

A catalogue record for this book is available
from the British Library.

ISBN 978–1–4448–3748–3

Published by
F. A. Thorpe (Publishing)
Anstey, Leicestershire

Set by Words & Graphics Ltd.
Anstey, Leicestershire
Printed and bound in Great Britain by
T. J. International Ltd., Padstow, Cornwall

This book is printed on acid-free paper

Acknowledgements

With thanks to Cara Cooper and Pia Fenton for their help and advice on this story.

1

'You'll have to start immediately,' said the agent, spreading her hands wide. 'The other girl was meant to start today, but that's very short notice for you, I suspect. Or can you go at the drop of a hat?'

Hazel Dobson contemplated the words of the recruitment agent. Only a week ago she'd given the woman her CV, stating that she was willing to take any secretarial position, as long as it took her back to her native Norfolk. Although she'd prefer to work in an industry relevant to the coursework she'd done at her evening classes, it wasn't essential.

She hadn't imagined that the girl the agency had originally hoped to place would break her leg, and that they would call on her so soon. But, she admitted to herself, the position sounded ideal, and the offer came at the right moment.

What she hadn't told the woman, because she didn't want to appear desperate, was that her current boss had started making passes at her. He kept finding excuses to stand a little too close to her, or to put his hand on her arm — or some other part of her anatomy. It made Hazel feel uncomfortable, but she needed the job so she'd put up with it.

However, when he'd contrived to lock them both inside the stationery cupboard, 'accidentally' losing the key in his pocket, and then tried to kiss her, Hazel had had enough. Now she just wanted to get as far away as possible.

'It's no problem,' she replied. 'I'm owed some holiday from my last job and wanted to take it at the end of my notice period, and my flatmate's already found someone else to move in from next week.' Running her fingers through her short brown hair, she laughed. 'In fact, I'm free as a bird.'

'Oh, good!' the agent exhaled. 'Gough Associates is a long-standing client of ours, and I placed quite a few people with them when they were based in London. Not so much since they relocated to Norfolk, but I didn't want to let them down.'

Searching her disorganised desk for the necessary paperwork, she handed Hazel a folder. 'It's all in there: salary, job description, working hours, perks, etc. A pretty good package, I'd say. The firm's run from Mr Gough's estate and they've agreed you can live in until you've found somewhere to rent. There are also instructions on how to get there. You'll need that, unless someone is willing to pick you up from the station.'

Hazel smiled. It was typical of Londoners to regard Norfolk as the back of beyond, but the chance to return to her roots after living half her life in the capital was a dream come true. 'I know the area quite well and should be able to find it. But thanks.'

'That's settled then. I'll ring them and let them know you'll be there tomorrow.'

'Tomorrow is perfect,' said Hazel. 'That'll give me time to pack and tell my friends where I'm going.'

'You're a real lifesaver, my dear. Best of luck.'

No, you're the lifesaver, Hazel thought, as she left the woman's office. She was itching to get out of London, and it would be wonderful to be nearer to Great-aunt Rose too.

* * *

Her confidence left her the next day, when she alighted at Combury Cross station, and there was no one to greet her. After she'd left the agent's office, Hazel had called the contact at Gough Associates to confirm that they were expecting her, and had been told someone would meet her at the station.

She glanced at her wristwatch. She'd left London for an agreed afternoon arrival, and had now been waiting for forty-five minutes. Annoyingly, there was still no sign of a car.

'Forgotten about you, have they?'

Hazel turned to the uniformed man behind her. The stationmaster, a kindly-looking gentleman with a greying beard and keen blue eyes, regarded her thoughtfully.

'It looks that way. Are there any buses at this time of day?'

She explained where she was going, and the man nodded, looking over her shoulder at the station clock. 'There's one coming in around about . . . now.'

Sure enough, just then a bus swung around the corner and stopped outside the station. With a sigh of relief, Hazel hoisted up her wheeled suitcase and large holdall to board the bus. Suddenly there was a tremendous bang, and black smoke belched out from the back of the vehicle.

'Dear me,' tutted the stationmaster. 'Sounds bad, that.'

'Sorry, love.' The bus driver, a

cheerful blonde woman, jumped down from the driver's seat. 'Doesn't look like I'll be going any further today.'

'Will there be a replacement soon?'

'Could be a fair while,' she replied, and pulled out her mobile phone to report the damage to the depot. 'You're better off getting a taxi.'

But there were no taxis available. In the end, and to stop the concerned stationmaster clucking around her like a mother hen, Hazel decided to walk.

'It's a couple of miles!' he protested. 'And it looks like rain.'

'I'll be fine,' Hazel reassured him, touched by his concern. 'I've got my map, and my two good feet. And a little rain never hurt anybody.' Pulling her suitcase along, she began to walk.

When she'd reached the outskirts of town, it started to rain, as the stationmaster had predicted. It wasn't the usual drizzle, which Norfolk was known for, but fat, heavy raindrops the size of raisins, which drummed a tattoo against her bags and the deserted road.

This could only happen to me, she thought glumly. *Hazel, the disaster magnet. The Bad Luck Charm, Calamity Jane. Give me a boat to steer, and I'll ram it into an iceberg.*

Resolutely, she pulled up the collar of her red trench coat and tied her scarf around her neck, glad that she'd chosen not to wear the jacket which might have been more appropriate for her first day at work.

However, her thin coat couldn't keep out the incessant rain, and in no time she was soaked to the skin. Shivering, she dug into her holdall for her umbrella, but it was a struggle to carry that and manage two heavy bags at the same time. When a sudden gust of wind blew it out of her hand and into the middle of the road, she dashed after it without thinking.

She screamed as a car screeched to a halt in front of her with only inches to spare.

★　★　★

Jonathan Gough frowned as he put down the phone. How typical of his colleague to always pass the buck. Tabitha Fanshawe was a brilliant architect, and Jonathan never doubted when he started up Gough Associates that she'd be an asset to the company. But, when she was working on a project, Tabitha also had a tendency to forget practical matters. Like yesterday, when she'd sworn she'd be available to pick up the new secretary from the station this afternoon, only to arrange a meeting with an important client at exactly the same time. And there was no one else in the office right now he could send instead.

Checking the wall clock in his office, Jonathan grabbed his car keys and his jacket. There was no way he'd make it in time to meet this girl off the train unless he ran every single red light and broke the speed limit, but hopefully she had enough sense to wait at the station for someone to pick her up.

He slammed the office door behind

him and called to his housekeeper, Mrs Whitmore. 'I'm picking up the new secretary from the station now. Is everything ready for her?'

Mrs Whitmore appeared in the doorway of what in the old days would have been considered the servants' quarters. 'Yes, Mr Gough. I've put her in the west wing. It's a bit cut off from the rest of the house, but the bathroom's modern and I think she'll be comfortable there.'

'Fine, excellent,' Jonathan called absent-mindedly over his shoulder. 'I'll be back shortly. If Robert Miles calls from Didcot Developments, please tell him I'm on it, and I'll get back to him as soon as possible. Don't let it go to answerphone; he hates that.'

'Of course, Mr Gough. Leave it with me.'

Smiling to himself, Jonathan crossed the gravelled drive in front of the house. He'd tried in vain to persuade the housekeeper to address him more informally — this was the twenty-first century, after all — but Irene Whitmore insisted on maintaining a respectful distance between them.

Unlocking the car with his key fob, he got in. The Land Rover was old, barely road-worthy, and strewn with papers, sweet wrappers and empty water bottles. On the back seat, which was covered in silky, golden dog hair, lay a half-eaten apple, all brown and shrivelled up now. He shook his head; he ought to tidy the car, but somehow simple tasks always got pushed to the back of the agenda. Running the company took up most of his time.

As he drove out through the heavy metal gates, which opened automatically, it started to rain. Flicking the windscreen wipers on full speed, Jonathan again bemoaned the fact that Tabitha had abandoned the poor secretary at the station and only informed him at the last minute. He envisaged himself in the new girl's shoes: if *he* had been forced to wait that long, he'd probably have found alternative means of transport. So the girl might not even be there when Jonathan arrived. And, if she'd taken the bus, the distance between the bus stop and the manor house was far enough for her to become completely drenched in this weather.

All in all, if first impressions mattered, Gough Associates would be presented in a very bad light.

Muttering to himself, he sped up as he rounded a bend in the road, then slammed on the brakes when something red flew into his field of vision. There was an awful screech as the Land Rover skidded along the wet tarmac and came to a stop almost sideways across the road. Heart thudding and with his knuckles white from gripping the steering wheel, Jonathan stared out into the driving rain.

In front of him, a small figure in red was standing stock-still, staring at him, wide-eyed, through the windscreen. It took him a moment or two, then

Jonathan sprang into action. He jumped out of the car and ran to the person on the road.

'What's the matter with you?' he yelled, more from shock than anger. 'You could've been killed!'

It was a woman, he saw that now. Petite, with short brown hair plastered to her skull and a rain-saturated scarf wrapped around her slender neck in a haphazard fashion, she looked like a drowned rat, although Jonathan had never actually seen one. She didn't reply, but kept staring at the Land Rover and the high wheel arch which was only inches from her chest.

Not knowing what else to do, Jonathan took her by the shoulders and shook her gently. 'Are you okay? I didn't hit you, did I?'

Finally her eyes focused on him, big brown eyes like a deer's, and she flung her arms around him, burying her head against his shoulder.

'Oh . . . oh, my goodness,' she cried. 'I thought this was the end!'

Jonathan gently extricated himself from this strange creature, who was at least a head shorter than him, and held her at arm's length, his hands still resting on her shoulders.

'Trust me, you're fine. I might be driving an old rust bucket, but the brakes are in perfect working order. I think we both got a bit of a fright, that's all.' He looked her up and down. 'What a stroke of luck you were wearing that red coat; I don't think I'd have seen you otherwise. Visibility is pretty bad.'

'I'm sorry. My umbrella, it, er, blew out of my hand, and . . . well, I didn't see you coming.'

'Not to worry, although if you want it back, you'll have to traipse across that muddy field over there.'

Jonathan inclined his head, and she looked in the direction he was nodding where the offending umbrella was dancing in the wind, almost as if it was challenging them to come and get it. Her eyes returned to his. Suddenly she smiled, and Jonathan experienced a peculiar jolt, as if someone had punched him in the stomach.

A smile to rival the sun, he thought.

'I'm wearing my best boots,' she said, with a wry grin, 'so I'll give that a miss. It was an old umbrella anyway.' As if she'd only just become aware of their closeness, she pulled away from his grasp and straightened her scarf.

'Listen, er, can I give you a lift somewhere? It's the least I can do after nearly sending you into the next world.'

'That's very kind of you.' Her beaming smile was back. 'I'm going to Combury Manor. Do you know it?'

'Do I know it? I own it! You must be the new secretary.'

'Oh? Yes, I suppose I am. Hazel Dobson. And you are . . . ?'

'Jonathan Gough, director of Gough Associates. Call me Jonathan.' He held out his hand to shake hers. 'I'll explain why I'm late, but let's get out of this rain first.'

In the car, after he'd stowed her bags in the boot, Jonathan apologised that no one had met her at the station. 'It was my partner, Tabitha's job to pick you up today but she was called away urgently, and I wasn't informed until later.' He smiled sheepishly. 'Sometimes the communication between myself and the other architects doesn't work so well. That's why we need a secretary. Someone to tell us off if we forget something important.'

'Tell you off, eh?' She glanced about her in the Land Rover and, spotting the half-eaten apple on the back seat, sent him an impish grin. 'Well, you might start by cleaning up your car.'

'Point taken. It's a bit of a tip, isn't it?' Jonathan reached back to pick up the apple, and tossed it out of the window.

'But not by littering,' she said sternly.

'It's 100% organic. I'm just planting another apple tree.'

As he turned the key in the ignition, their eyes met again. Hazel Dobson was smiling, the sort of smile which reached all the way to her doe-like eyes, and

Jonathan felt suffused by warmth. When he had to look away and concentrate on his driving, it was as if a spell had been broken.

She was quiet while they drove, seemingly lost in thought, and it gave Jonathan a chance to study her out of the corner of his eye. She wasn't conventionally pretty. Aside from her unusually large brown eyes, she had pale pixie features, and her short brown hair, which was now drying off inside the car, was cut in a cool, modern style like that of so many other girls.

Plain Jane, he thought, but immediately revised his opinion. There was something extraordinary about those pixie features. It was as if she'd just stepped out of a computer animated children's film; not quite real, but real enough to be believable. And her smile made her more alive to him than any other woman he'd ever met. He found himself strangely attracted to her and wondered what was going through her head right now, what she thought of him.

Then he checked himself and focused on the road.

Don't go there, Jonathan. Remember what happened last time.

★ ★ ★

Why does he have to be so good-looking? Hazel's former boss had been very attractive — she might even have liked him if he hadn't been so slimy — but he wasn't a patch on the man beside her. Her heart fluttered a little when she appraised him under her lowered lashes, carefully without giving anything away.

Jonathan Gough was tall and gangly, a bit on the thin side perhaps, with slender hands, brilliant blue eyes and a thatch of strawberry-blond hair flopping over his brow. He didn't look anything like she'd imagined a successful and renowned architect to be. He wasn't suave, sophisticated or dressed

17

in a designer suit; instead, he seemed a little untidy and distracted, as if he needed someone to organise him. If his summary of her new job was anything to go by, 'organising him' would be one of her tasks.

Heat rose to her cheeks when she recalled how she'd flung herself into his arms. Okay, it was the shock that had made her do it, but even so. And then she'd proceeded to grin like a monkey at everything he said. Why couldn't she be more aloof?

She wished she was one of those girls who always stayed cool, but instead she was ruled by her emotions and would often speak without thinking first. Well, she'd have to find a way to keep them in check this time.

Otherwise, this could get complicated, and complications were the last thing Hazel needed right now.

2

When they drove through the wrought-iron gates to Combury Manor, Hazel's misgivings were replaced by awe. The rain had subsided to a proper Norfolk drizzle, and the red brick building could be seen in all its splendour against a sliver of blue sky. Three storeys high, with gabled wings on either side of the main house, a balustraded roof and an imposing front porch with twisted columns, it had a grand but welcoming air about it.

'What a beautiful house! I'm going to love working here!' she exclaimed without thinking, then felt her cheeks heat up when she realised how gauche she must sound.

Jonathan didn't seem to have noticed. He pressed a remote control which lay on the dashboard, and the gates closed behind them. 'I hope so. Our last admin person retired a few weeks ago, and it hasn't been easy finding a replacement. Probably because we're tucked out of the way like this.' He cast her a sideways glance. 'I hope the isolation won't get to you; most young women would want to be nearer to Norwich, I should think.'

'Not at all. I was never much of a townie. My flatmate was forever out partying, while I preferred being at home.' She laughed. 'She probably thought I was the most boring person ever.'

'Boring? Surely not.'

Hazel felt Jonathan's eyes on her as he parked the Land Rover just outside the front porch, and her neck prickled with self-consciousness. He was having a peculiar effect on her, and she racked her brains for a safer subject.

'Combury Manor is built in the Jacobean style, isn't it?' she asked. 'Although the porch looks more Georgian or Palladian with those columns.'

'You have a good eye. Most people would've said Elizabethan. It was built in 1659 by a wealthy lace-maker, a man who'd worked himself up in the industry. His grandson added the porch later, I believe. It seemed appropriate when I bought it because, like the lace-maker, I started my company from scratch, and now there's eight of us. Nine, including you.'

He got out of the car and moved around to the other side where he opened the door for Hazel and held an umbrella over her. She blushed furiously at the gentlemanly gesture, something she wasn't used to, and busied herself with her handbag to hide her embarrassment.

'Thank you,' she whispered, as she got under the shelter of his umbrella. 'You're very kind.'

'You're soaked to the skin, and it's my fault. What sort of employer would I be if I didn't at least try to make amends?'

Hazel didn't have an answer to that. Sheltering her against the drizzle, Jonathan saw her safely to the porch, handed her the umbrella, then returned to the car to fetch her bags. She took the opportunity to study the porch area, which projected about nine feet out from the main building. Above the doorway, a coat of arms and monogram was carved into the stone — presumably, the industrious lace-maker must have been knighted later — and over the twisted columns on either side of the wide door were two robed, mythological figures in niches.

From what she could see, the building and grounds were well-maintained, with neatly-clipped holly hedges on either side of the house enclosing the gardens at the back, and carefully pruned oak trees, now devoid of leaves, lining the drive.

It must cost a fortune to maintain, she thought. Jonathan's company might be thriving, but surely no one, no matter how successful, could afford to buy a place like this unless there was family money involved. Hazel felt as if she was in the presence of royalty.

'You own all this?' She couldn't suppress the note of wonder which had crept into her voice.

'Mm, yes and no.' Jonathan grimaced. 'The building society has the greatest stake in it, obviously, and my father owns a part of it too. The outbuildings — in other words, the stables, workshops, and such — are used by small companies, so I get some rental income from that, and the whole of the ground floor of the main building is taken up by the company. My partner, Tabitha, has a share in that.'

'Oh.' Hazel wondered what, precisely, he meant by the word 'partner'. Was this Tabitha person his girlfriend, or fiancée perhaps? She knew that nowadays many couples chose not to marry, although that concept was completely alien to her.

Balancing her bags, Jonathan opened the door for her with a wry grin. 'Did you think I was rich?'

That was exactly what she had been thinking. However, she didn't want him to get the impression that she was after him, whether he was rich or not — she wasn't, absolutely not! — so she merely shrugged.

'It's not every day you get to meet the lord of the manor.'

Jonathan laughed. 'I'm no lord. I'm just an ordinary man who likes to work in beautiful surroundings. Ah, there's Mrs Whitmore, my housekeeper. Come and say hello.'

A middle-aged woman, with a soft grey perm and a cook's apron, appeared at the foot of a large staircase as they entered the grand hallway. She smiled when she saw Hazel, then her expression changed to a look of utter dismay.

'Oh, my word! Look at you! Soaked to the skin, you poor thing. Mr Gough!' She turned to her employer with a frown.

'I know. I should've been there on time. Sadly I wasn't, and Hazel Dobson here decided to walk.'

Mrs Whitmore was clearly a formidable woman, and Hazel felt a little sorry for Jonathan; technically it wasn't his fault she'd been rained on. 'It's nothing,' she assured the older woman. 'If I can just go somewhere and change, I'll be fine.'

'Of course,' said the housekeeper. 'I'll show you to your room and let you get settled, then we can discuss practical matters later.'

She took the smaller of Hazel's two bags and began to climb the carved oak staircase. 'Your client called, as you expected, Mr Gough. He'd appreciate it if you could drive by his office tonight.'

'Ah.' Running his hands through his fair hair, Jonathan's eyes met Hazel's. 'Duty calls, I'm afraid. I'd hoped we could get to know each other better before I introduce you to everyone else, but it'll have to wait until tomorrow now.'

'Tomorrow is fine,' she reassured him, while she wondered at his ambiguous choice of words.

Jonathan disappeared through a door leading off the hallway. Hazel followed Mrs Whitmore up the stairs and through what seemed like a labyrinth of corridors and narrow oak-panelled passages, until they stopped outside a heavy door. Mrs Whitmore produced a key from her apron pocket, unlocked the door, then handed the key to Hazel.

'This is what we call the west wing, although it's a rather grand word for a simple apartment. The nanny used to live here, but that was a couple of years ago.'

'Nanny?'

'Mr Gough has two children, Miss Dobson.'

Children? Hazel had wondered about Tabitha's role in Jonathan's life, but it hadn't occurred to her that he could be a father as well. He'd made no reference to that himself, which she found puzzling.

'Where are the children now?'

'They're away at boarding school.'

Mrs Whitmore sniffed, and Hazel had a feeling the housekeeper didn't approve, so she didn't enquire further.

Curiosity killed the cat, she reminded

herself. No doubt everything would be revealed in good time.

'You have your own private bathroom, bedroom and a small sitting room, as well as a kitchenette, although you're welcome to eat in the kitchen with me, at seven. I'd appreciate the company.' Mrs Whitmore put her hand on Hazel's arm. 'I was so glad when I heard you were to live in for a while. This place could do with a bit of life in it.'

Handing Hazel a map of the house, she explained the way to the kitchen, how to find the laundry room, the main office, and the door to the gardens, then left Hazel to change and unpack.

★ ★ ★

Steering the Land Rover towards Norwich, Jonathan contemplated the project he was currently working on.

Robert Miles was a local entrepreneur, a so-called mover and shaker, who was constructing a call centre on the outskirts of Norwich. He'd engaged Gough Associates to draw up the blueprints and a local construction company for the actual building work, and although Jonathan was delighted to be involved in a project which would bring jobs to the region, it hadn't been without a number of hitches.

This time it was a planning permission issue, which Jonathan hoped to straighten out with a revised set of drawings.

Thinking of architecture brought him back to Hazel Dobson. It surprised him that she was so knowledgeable about the Jacobean style of building, but there was no reason why she shouldn't be.

'What did you expect?' he muttered to himself. 'A blonde bimbo?'

His prejudices about her profession shamed him, and he vowed to make up for it. There were plenty of books on the subject of Jacobean and Elizabethan architecture in his library, and he decided to find them for her. He could just imagine her enthusiasm.

His face split into a grin when he realised that he was going to enjoy basking in that beaming smile of hers. He recalled how enticing it had been to feel her delicate frame in his arms when she'd buried her head against his shoulder, and how he'd delighted in the scent of apple shampoo from her newly-washed hair. It had been a long time since he'd held a woman like that.

Then his circumstances brought him back to reality. *Careful, Jonathan.*

* * *

Shortly before seven o'clock, Hazel found her way through the seemingly vast building to the kitchen. Large and traditional, with an Aga in the chimney space and copper pots suspended from ceiling hooks, it was painted a warm primrose yellow with matching café curtains and chair cushions. Delicious smells wafted from a cast-iron dish on the hob, and a chubby marmalade cat was stretched out on the floor in front of the cooker, eyeing her lazily. Hazel immediately felt at home, and she bent to stroke the cat.

'Something smells wonderful.'

'I hope you like lamb. We need something hearty on a day like this.' The housekeeper was spreading a brightly-coloured tablecloth over a scrubbed pine table at the far end of the kitchen.

'I can think of nothing better.' That explained the mouth-watering smells. Hazel was already feeling warmer at the prospect. 'Do you need any help, Mrs Whitmore?'

'You can finish laying the table. Crockery is in that cupboard over there.' Mrs Whitmore pointed to an enormous dresser which took up an entire wall. 'And you'll find knives and forks in the drawer. Set the table for three. Oh, and please call me Irene. No need to stand on ceremony around here.'

'Okay . . . Irene. And I'd love for you to call me Hazel.' She thought for a moment. 'Although I did notice that you call Jonathan *Mr Gough*.'

Smoothing down the tablecloth, Irene sent her an amused look. 'There are certainly no flies on you, my young friend. Yes, I address him as Mr Gough. With some people, formality is best observed, which you'll probably discover for yourself soon enough.'

Irene returned to the stove, and Hazel finished setting the table. Considering Irene's cryptic words about formality, she wondered about the third person who was to eat with them since Jonathan was out with his client. Most likely another member of staff. An estate this size would require more than just a housekeeper to run it.

Her unvoiced question was answered when a gust of wind indicated that an outside door had been opened, and her eyes turned to the scullery just off the large kitchen. A man shook the rain off his oilskin jacket, then discarded his muddy Wellington boots in an untidy heap on the flagstone floor.

'Here's George,' said Irene.

The newcomer entered the kitchen. Judging him to be in his late sixties, Hazel took in his threadbare tweed jacket, faded corduroys, and now a pair of carpet slippers which had seen better days. With a shock of fine white hair standing out in all directions and a preoccupied frown, he resembled a mad scientist and not the groundsman or gardener which he appeared to be.

He gave a curt nod to Irene, then started when his eyes fell on Hazel, who was just about to step forward and greet him formally. She stopped in her tracks, and her smile froze.

The man named George was staring at her with undisguised hostility.

'Who are you?' he demanded.

'Now, now, George,' said Irene, as she spooned out steaming hot stew. 'Easy does it. This is Hazel Dobson, Mr Gough's new secretary. She's just arrived from London, no doubt exhausted from her long journey, so there's no need for you to scare the poor girl away with your gruff ways, is there?'

George frowned. 'Hm, s'pose not. What's for dinner?'

'Your favourite. Lamb casserole.'

He seemed to cheer at that and, pulling out a chair, he sat down at the table just as Irene placed a plate of stew and fluffy white potatoes in front of him. Without another word, he tucked in, wolfing down his food as if he hadn't eaten in days. Now Hazel came to think of it, he had a certain scrawny and ravenous look about him.

All the while he kept casting Hazel suspicious glances.

What did I do? she wondered. Deciding to ignore him, she engaged Irene in conversation about the estate and Jonathan's company. The housekeeper was only too happy to talk, and Hazel was soon able to forget the gardener's animosity.

In record time, George had finished his stew and Irene dished him up another helping. 'You're too thin,

George. Did you skip lunch again?'

'Can't remember.'

'You work too hard. Why don't you ease up for a day or two? Surely the grounds don't need that much attention in this weather.'

'Work's not going to do itself.'

'Of course not, but — ' Irene continued, but he cut her off.

'I wish you'd stop fussing so! I'm not a child that needs to be molly-coddled or wrapped in cotton wool!'

Having delivered the longest speech since he entered the kitchen, George rose from the table with an exasperated expression, mumbled an apology, and disappeared into the bowels of the large house carrying his plate, his old carpet slippers slapping against the tiled floor.

Irene sighed. 'You mustn't take any notice of George. At heart he's the kindest person you're ever likely to meet, but he's had a run of bad luck, and I'm afraid it's turned him sour.'

'What happened?'

'Oh, it's a long story, and I don't

want to bore you.'

'If I'm going to be working with him, it might be helpful to know the details. And just so you know, I'm not a gossip.'

'I didn't think you were.' Irene smiled. 'All right. Let me just clear up first and make some coffee, then we can chat.'

Together they tidied the kitchen. When they were settled at the table again, with a pot of coffee and a plate of biscuits, Irene told her George's story.

'His company, a biological research facility, had liquidity problems and went bankrupt. The administrators who took over arranged for the shares in the company to be sold to the highest bidder, as always when a company goes into administration.' Irene paused to take a sip of her coffee. 'What George hadn't reckoned with was his old business partner making an extremely low offer to the administrators for the shares, and buying all of them for a song — even George's half — then starting up in business on his own the next day with all the stock.'

'Is that legal?'

Irene nodded. 'There was nothing George could do. He lost everything: money, premises, years of research. It broke him, I'm afraid. That's why he doesn't trust people now.'

'That's terrible!'

Hazel felt her stomach contract at the thought of how devastating it must have been for the older man. He hadn't made a favourable impression on her, but she understood him a little better now and vowed that she'd try to befriend him. If he'd let her.

But Irene hadn't finished. 'Fortunately, George still had his share of Combury Manor. Because of some legal wrangling that I don't quite understand, the administrators weren't able to touch that.'

'Sorry, you've confused me now,' said Hazel. 'George has a share in the manor? Jonathan mentioned that his father had a share but he didn't mention anyone else.'

'George *is* Mr Gough's father. Didn't he tell you?'

'No.' Hazel shook her head. He hadn't told her about his children either, and it puzzled her. Why the big secret?

'Fortunately, Mr Gough needed a gardener for the estate,' Irene explained. 'It keeps George busy and stops him from brooding too much, and it's a great help for me to have a handyman around, to change light bulbs I can't reach and take the rubbish out, that sort of thing. My back's not what it was.'

They'd finished their coffee, and Hazel rose to clear away the cups. 'You must tell me if there's anything I can do to help.'

'Oh, no.' Irene waved her hand dismissively. 'You'll be busy with the architects. They're a disorganised lot. Besides, my daughter Alison comes in once a week to do the heavy cleaning. Between us, we manage.'

The housekeeper fed the cat, then

they bid each other goodnight. Hazel confessed that she was nervous about the following day.

'I'm sure you'll get on just fine,' Irene reassured her, but she didn't look at Hazel when she said it.

★   ★   ★

Back in her small apartment, Hazel got ready for bed then pulled back the heavy curtains so she could look at the night sky while lying down; she'd never been able to do that in London, because of the proximity to her neighbours.

She noticed a peculiar green light at the far end of the grounds, almost indiscernible among the naked trees. Her first thought was that someone in one of the rented outbuildings was working late, then she remembered that the outbuildings were all on the east side of the house.

There must be another building at the end of the grounds, she concluded, although it seemed impractical to her.

Her last thought before her exhausted head hit the pillow was the strange colour of the light. Why was it green?

3

She didn't have time to dwell on the mysterious light. The following day started with a hasty breakfast in the kitchen with Irene, then a tour of the office with Jonathan.

In contrast to the rest of the manor house, which was oak-panelled and furnished in a style befitting an earlier period, the main office took up most of the ground floor and was open-plan, light and airy, with adjustable desks and chairs in two rows down the sides like in a school room. Drawings and blueprints were pinned to noticeboards, and art materials were strewn about the place. It seemed efficient yet disorderly at the same time, and Hazel couldn't wait to start.

The other architects hadn't arrived yet, and Jonathan showed her where everything was. There was so much to remember that she felt she was being dropped in at the deep end, but his presence and his apparent faith in her abilities to manage the office were reassuring.

'What made you take a job in such a remote area?' he asked.

'It isn't really remote for me. I come from Norfolk originally, but my parents moved to London when I was young. Sadly, they're both dead now.'

'I'm sorry to hear that.'

Hazel swallowed back the tears which often threatened when she spoke of her parents. The pain of their deaths in a traffic accident three years earlier was still raw, but she'd learnt to deal with it.

'My only living relative is my great-aunt Rose, who lives in Combury Cross,' Hazel explained. 'She used to come to London to see me, but sadly she's been confined to a wheelchair and is in a nursing home. Finding a job so close to where she lives was just perfect.'

'It's perfect for me too.'

There was a curious expression in Jonathan's eyes which Hazel couldn't quite decipher. Fresh from the shower, he smelled irresistibly of soap and aftershave, and with his shirtsleeves rolled up to his elbows, Hazel noticed the muscles on his strong forearms flexing every time he moved. She had to stuff her hands in her pockets to stop herself from reaching out and touching him.

What am *I* *thinking?* she chided herself, and forced the conversation back on neutral ground.

'I've enjoyed living in London,' she continued. 'I probably wouldn't have had the same opportunities to go to college if I'd stayed here. There's so much on offer there, and the firm of architects I worked for previously, let me have time off for my exams.'

She didn't mention that her immediate boss had grumbled and said something rude and derogatory about how education was wasted on women. He had then added, lewdly, that women belonged in the bedroom, with a look in his eyes that made Hazel's skin crawl. She couldn't imagine Jonathan expressing a similar sentiment, but she'd been wrong about people before.

'I expect you're longing to visit your aunt.'

'I'll go as soon as I can. Although,' she shot him a cautious look, 'I wouldn't do that without running it by you first.'

'Your time is yours. We might not keep regular hours here when we're working on a project, but I'm sure you can see your aunt during the day which is probably the best time to visit an elderly person. You can always make up the hours later.'

'Thank you.'

'I may be the boss, Hazel, but I'm not an ogre. You seem to think that I would be. Any particular reason why?'

He smiled down at her, and her breath caught in her throat. It would be so easy to tell him about her previous boss, but she decided to err on the side of caution. She didn't know him that well yet.

'No reason,' she replied, and changed the subject. 'I met your father last night. He seemed surprised to see me.'

'Ah, yes, my father.' Grimacing, Jonathan ran his hand through his fair hair. 'I told him you were coming, but it must've slipped his mind. Communication isn't great between us really.'

'I understand he works on the estate grounds. Isn't he a little old for that?' The pathetic image of George, with his flyaway hair and carpet slippers, had stayed in her mind.

Jonathan sent her a sharp look, although a smile tugged at the corners of his mouth. 'You're very direct, aren't you?'

'Is that a bad thing?'

'No, it's . . . refreshing.'

He eyed her for a moment, another inscrutable look on his face, and Hazel felt herself go hot under his stare. She met his eyes as far as she dared, reminding herself yet again that complications were the last thing she needed.

They were interrupted by the arrival of the other employees. Soon the office was buzzing with the sound of good-natured banter, printers whirring and mugs clinking. It reminded her of her previous workplace before everything had gone pear-shaped with her manager.

Jonathan made the introductions, and they all welcomed Hazel enthusiastically. The majority of them were men, in casual clothes and of different ages, but there was one woman among them. Dressed in an exotic, flowing kaftan, Ellie was big-boned, with large, expressive hands. A pair of spectacles hung from a chain around her neck and a hair clip, shaped like a sunflower, tried unsuccessfully to tame her frizzy hair. She pulled Hazel aside.

'We're very glad to have you here. The office is in a bit of state. But don't tell the big boss I said that or I'll be in the doghouse.' She gave Hazel a conspiratorial wink.

'I won't breathe a word.'

'Joking aside, it's a great place to work. Everyone's friendly and helpful. Well, almost everyone,' Ellie added, but didn't elaborate. 'Just give me a shout if there's anything you don't understand.'

Jonathan's voice cut through the chatter. 'Right, enough loitering. Robert Miles wants to see a revised set of drawings by Monday, so there's no time to waste. It's vital that we keep this contract.'

This was followed by a chorus of groans, but people returned to their desks readily enough although the buzz continued.

'Tabitha here yet?' Jonathan asked.

'No,' replied a dark-haired man in his thirties.

Another employee rolled his eyes, but looked away when Jonathan frowned at him.

'She's probably running late,' Ellie commented neutrally, although even a newcomer like Hazel could hear the unspoken word 'again' hanging in the air.

Jonathan nodded pensively. 'You're probably right.'

He disappeared into his own office at the far end, which Hazel knew also doubled as a small meeting room. Extremely aware of the exhilarating yet unsettling effect he had on her, she was quite relieved that he'd left. But she found it required all the self-control she possessed to force the thought of him from her mind as she sat down at the desk she'd been allocated and set to work.

★ ★ ★

The morning passed in a flash. By lunchtime, Hazel had made significant inroads into the teetering pile of papers on her desk and filed away most of them. Lunch was a happy, slightly chaotic affair. Some of the employees left for the village pub, while others, including Ellie, ate their packed lunch around a table by the office coffee machine. Irene had prepared a plate of

47

sandwiches in the kitchen for those living in, and had told Hazel to help herself, so she quickly selected a few, as well as some fruit, then joined the others.

Jonathan stayed in his office throughout, the door closed firmly behind him. Through the glass partition, Hazel could see that he was on the phone.

When lunch was over, she realised that she hadn't enjoyed herself so much in years. Her colleagues had treated her as an equal, and they'd quickly established that they had a lot in common.

Certain she was going to like working in her new environment, she returned to her filing.

When there was a lull in activity, she had a chance to study her colleagues hard at work. The architects at Gough Associates were a varied bunch, but they were all incredibly creative and skilled, particularly Ellie. Her large, fleshy hands were able to produce the most delicate drawings.

'I wish I could draw like that,' Hazel commented, when her duties took her past Ellie's desk. 'You're amazing!'

'You're very sweet, but I know my limitations. I'm only average. Come, let me show you something.' Ellie climbed down from her high chair and led Hazel to a desk at the end of the room, the only one not yet occupied. 'Tabitha Fanshawe sits here,' she said, and pointed to a work-in-progress on the drawing board.

Stepping closer, Hazel felt her jaw drop. In a strong, confident hand, the artist had created a building with both modern and traditional touches, rendered in wood as well as concrete, steel and glass, enclosed by a garden and discreet car park. Grey-shaded high-rises on either side made it jump out and come to life, giving the illusion of an oasis in a forbidding city-scape. Other drawings, equally bold and self-assured, hung on a noticeboard above the desk.

'She's good, isn't she?'

Speechless with awe and envy, Hazel nodded.

'That's the only reason Jonathan tolerates her tardiness. You don't come across that kind of ability every day.'

Ellie was right. She might be a skilled architect herself, but the elusive Tabitha's drawings were quite simply stunning.

Just like the woman herself.

The familiar buzz in the office died as the door opened and a woman entered. Tabitha Fanshawe was tall, with flowing blonde hair and long, slim legs. She was dressed in a figure-hugging, green velvet jacket, a crisp white shirt, and designer jeans. Stiletto crocodile skin boots partly explained her impressive height. A matching handbag hung over her arm and, with her perfect skin, baby-blue eyes, and lips curved like a Cupid's bow, it was as if Tabitha had just stepped off the catwalk.

She was the most beautiful woman Hazel had ever met — she'd seen quite a few glamorous people when living in London — and she couldn't stop staring, mouth wide open, utterly spellbound.

A fug of expensive perfume preceded Tabitha, and Ellie's demonstrative sneeze brought Hazel back to reality. She smiled and held out her hand.

'Hi, I'm Hazel Dobson, the new secretary. We were just admiring your work. I hope you don't mind.'

Tabitha didn't take the hand. Instead, her eyes travelled up and down Hazel insultingly. Hazel felt her neck growing hot with embarrassment and indignation, and withdrew her hand.

'You're not very big, are you?' said Tabitha, at last. Her voice was low and throaty, and Hazel half-expected her to hiss.

Oh, like that, is it? she thought waspishly. *Well, two can play that game.* She stuck her chin out. 'It's not the size of the dog in the fight but the size of the fight in the dog that counts,' she replied.

Raising her finely sculpted eyebrows, Tabitha gave a little laugh. 'What's this: *The World According to Hazel Dobson, secretary?*'

'Actually, it's a quote from General Eisenhower.'

'Ooh, a history buff.' Tabitha put a French manicured fingernail against her dimpled cheek, a pose she'd no doubt practised in the mirror. 'Problem is, we need an office girl, not a professor. And you can start by getting me a cup of coffee.'

Behind her, Hazel heard Ellie gasp in outrage. The rule in the office was that everyone got their own coffee and offered everyone else while they were making it.

'And not from the coffee machine either,' Tabitha continued. 'That'll be stewed by now. I want it fresh from the kitchen, in a cup and saucer, one sugar cube, and hot milk in a little jug on the side. I'm sure that's something even a history buff can manage.'

'I wasn't told that was part of my

duties,' Hazel replied, while seething inside, 'so perhaps I should just go and check that with the boss?'

Changing tactics, Tabitha pouted prettily and fluttered her eyelashes. 'Aw, you wouldn't begrudge me a proper cup of coffee, would you? Only, I work best with the right kind of fuel inside me. Jonathan can vouch for that.'

She swanned off to her seat, apparently not expecting a reply. At the mention of Jonathan's name, Hazel decided to let it drop, reminding herself that she needed this job if she wanted to be near Aunt Rose. If that meant putting up with someone like Tabitha, then so be it.

★   ★   ★

Irene was in the kitchen chatting to a young woman with short, blonde hair, who was cradling the cat on her lap. Hazel recognised her from somewhere although she couldn't immediately place her.

'Hazel, this is my daughter, Alison.' Irene was stirring something on the stove. Sharp, fruity aromas rose from the pot, and a dozen clean jam jars were lined up on the kitchen island.

'Hi, there.' Alison gave a little wave. 'I've come to do the cleaning. You settling in all right?'

Smiling back, Hazel twigged. 'You're the bus driver, aren't you?'

'Yeah, that's my other job. I do the route that goes past the manor, and if you ever need a door-to-door service, just give me a ring on the mobile and I'll pick you up.' She grinned. 'Except Fridays, which is when I help Mum out. It was Jonathan's suggestion, when he saw how she was struggling getting the hoover up the stairs.'

'I wasn't struggling,' Irene protested, 'and it's Mr Gough to you.'

'Jonathan,' Alison shot back.

Rolling her eyes, Irene wiped her hands on her apron. 'What can I do for you, Hazel?'

'I need to make a pot of coffee, if that's all right.'

'Certainly. Let me show you where everything is.'

Irene showed Hazel how to use the electric coffee grinder and where to find coffee, sugar and milk, then she returned to her jam-making. Hazel quickly assembled a tray with everything requested by Tabitha, placing it all as neatly as possible, even adding a paper doily she'd found in a drawer. She wanted to make sure that Tabitha couldn't find fault with her.

Even so, it was tempting to replace the sugar in the bowl with salt.

'I see you've met Tabby-cat,' Alison commented.

'Alison,' Irene admonished.

'I don't care what you say, Mum. Tabby-cat is a right . . . ' she bit her lip, 'whatever. Anyway, I think she fancies herself as lady of the manor, and if Jonathan does decide to marry her, I don't think you'll like it here either.'

With a sigh, Irene nodded. 'I suppose

in that eventuality, I'd probably look for another position.'

'See?' Depositing the disgruntled cat on the floor, Alison rose from the chair to hold the door open for Hazel. As they passed in the doorway, Alison added in a low voice, 'Take my advice. Watch. Your. Back.'

4

It was as if Alison had known what would happen next.

Returning to the office with the coffee tray, Hazel was about to place it on a side table next to Tabitha's drawing board when the other woman carelessly flung a drawing onto the table, as if she hadn't seen Hazel there at all. The pot overbalanced, and coffee spilled all over the exquisite drawing.

'Oh no!' Shocked, Hazel began to dab at the drawing with the paper doily, only for the inks to run into a single, drab-coloured smudge.

Tabitha snatched the paper doily out of her hand. 'You stupid girl! Look what you've done! If we don't get the Robert Miles contract, it'll be all your fault.'

Hazel felt tears welling up in her eyes, and she swallowed hard to hold them back. 'I'm so sorry. I didn't expect you to put something on that table just as I was putting the tray down.'

'Are you saying it's my fault? Where, exactly, am I supposed to put my finished work to dry? Should I dangle it in the air perhaps?'

'No, of course not, I . . . '

The commotion had summoned their colleagues, including Jonathan, who gathered around the desk. 'What's going on?'

Tabitha flung her arm out with a theatrical sob. 'Look what she did! Hours of work, completely ruined. I'm devastated!'

'Hardly hours,' said Jonathan dryly. 'But never mind, I've got a copy. Let me just fetch it. You can work from there.'

He disappeared into his office and returned a moment later with the exact same drawing Tabitha had been working on, apart from the few extra lines she'd added that day.

'You keep copies of my work?' Tabitha looked astounded.

'Let's just call it a necessary back-up measure. You're hardly known for your punctuality.'

'But, Jonathan ... Jon-nee ... ' Tabitha sent him a wobbly smile, 'the meeting last night just carried on and on. I was so tired this morning.'

This earned a disgusted snort from Ellie.

Jonathan ignored Ellie's rudeness. 'I understand. That's why I keep copies of everyone's work, in case someone else has to pick it up at short notice. You're with me here, Tabs, aren't you?'

She nodded.

'And next time, get your own coffee.'

'Yes, Jonathan, I will. Sorry, Hazel, it was wrong of me to have a go at you. No harm done, right?'

Tabitha's baby-blue eyes widened fetchingly, but Hazel caught the calculating gleam as soon as Jonathan's back was turned.

'A word in your ear, if you don't mind.' Jonathan touched Hazel lightly on the arm.

'Of course.' She followed him into his office. *Job Centre, here I come*, she thought morosely.

It was the first time she'd actually been inside his private office, and despite her worry that he was about to give her the sack, she was curious. It was crammed with overflowing book-cases, a desk placed sideways to the glass partition which separated him from the main office, and a couple of chairs. Behind the desk hung a busy noticeboard, but the desk itself was tidy with only a lamp and a giant blotter on it. In the centre of the blotter someone, presumably Jonathan, had written down four numbers and then circled them.

Craning her neck, Hazel read '1572'. Wondering if this was the PIN code for his bank card, which would be a little careless, she looked away and tried to forget what she'd seen.

Jonathan closed the door behind them and sat down on the edge of his desk, indicating for Hazel to take one of the chairs.

'I know Tabitha isn't easy to work with,' he said, without preamble. 'She's used to getting her own way, but at heart she's kind and caring. I — we — need her on this project, so please try to get on.'

'I intend to.'

'Good. It would mean a lot to me.'

Jonathan's gaze met hers for a moment, and he raked his fingers through his hair. It was the same gesture he'd used when she'd mentioned his father's reaction to her, and one she'd come to equate with uncertainty. It made him appear slightly vulnerable, and Hazel knew in her heart that she'd do anything not to disappoint him.

At the same time, she couldn't help wondering if perhaps he was wrong about his beautiful partner. Hazel had seen no evidence of softness.

The day got progressively worse. Tabitha asked Hazel to do a number of menial tasks, the majority not in her job description, but — recalling Jonathan's concern — Hazel gritted her teeth and got on with it.

'Oh, and could you pick up my dry cleaning in town?' Tabitha asked airily. 'It's a jacket I need for a meeting tonight, but I haven't got the time to go myself.'

'I haven't got the time either, with all this other stuff you've asked me to do!' Hazel snapped.

'There's no need to take that tone with me. I only asked.'

'And I only replied.'

'I'll go.' An architect named Patrick stepped in. 'Hazel hasn't got a car, and I need to pop into town myself anyway. It'll save her the trip.'

'Take her with you then,' Tabitha pouted.

Patrick shrugged. 'What's the point of that? She's got enough to be getting on with. Just give me the ticket.'

Although she could hardly complain, Tabitha handed Patrick her dry cleaning stub with a vicious glare. He left, winking at Hazel, and she had to bite her lip to prevent a smile. There was no point in antagonising Tabitha further.

By the end of the day she was so tired she could barely eat the delicious pasta Irene had prepared. Sensing her less than buoyant mood, Irene dismissed her offer of help with the dishes and sent her to bed. There was no sign of George, and Jonathan didn't appear for supper either.

As she undressed, Hazel noticed the strange light again. This time it seemed to flicker, as if someone was walking back and forth in front of it. It made her think of an adventure story she'd read as a child, about smugglers signalling to ships with a lantern, but Jonathan's estate was inland and surrounded by endless fields. There was no one to signal to, surely?

There was bound to be a perfectly logical explanation, one that had nothing to do with romantic notions about smugglers delivering contraband goods. Hazel decided to investigate the grounds at the first given opportunity, if only to rein in her wild imaginings.

Then again, perhaps she was just seeing things because she was tired.

★   ★   ★

She rewarded herself with a lie-in on Saturday morning, then called Aunt Rose's nursing home, where the staff informed her that the residents were out on a day trip. Her aunt would love to see her the following day, they said, and Hazel confirmed that would fit in well with her plans.

After breakfast in her kitchenette, which the ever-thoughtful Irene had stocked up the day before, she put on her red coat and boots and found the access to the enclosed gardens on the map of the house.

The incessant drizzle had finally stopped, and the air was cold and damp. A heavy smell of mulch greeted her as she made her way down one of the gravelled paths of the formally laid-out garden. She slowed her pace for a moment to fill her lungs, realising how much she'd missed the country air. A blackbird hopped along in a flower bed beside her, overturning soggy leaves in its quest for worms.

At the end of the formal garden, a gap in the wall led to the park itself, and Hazel headed for where she'd calculated the green light originated.

That was as far as she got. From out of nowhere, a furry bolt rammed into her. She fell to the ground and held up her hands to fight off the muddy paws and rough tongue which seemed to assault her from all corners.

'Lulu, no!'

'Bad dog! Get off!'

The huge ball of fluff was hauled off her while two young voices scolded it.

Still winded, Hazel lay on the damp grass, rejoicing that she still appeared to be in one piece. A young boy appeared in her field of vision.

'Here, let me help you up, miss.' Without waiting for an answer, he grabbed Hazel's hand and unceremoniously pulled her upright. 'Sorry about Lulu. I took the lead off her because I didn't think anyone was here.'

Hazel rose and began to brush down her coat, then realised the futility of it. She was covered in mud, grass and white dog hairs. Sighing, she looked at the children. They were identical twins, that was obvious, with cow-licked brown hair, freckles, and bright blue eyes; perhaps nine or ten years old.

'I'm Seth,' said the boy who'd helped her to her feet. He pointed to the other boy, who was restraining a huge Golden Retriever. 'This is my brother, Ben. And that's Lulu.'

Whining, Lulu wagged her tail furiously and tried to pull free, but Ben had a firm grip on her, which was impressive, given the dog's size.

'She wants to say hello,' explained Seth.

'Hello,' said Hazel, cautiously eyeing the enormous beast.

'Proper hello. Sit, Lulu.'

Tongue lolling, the dog sat down on its rear, and Seth placed Hazel's hand on her silky head. 'She won't bite. Say you're sorry, Lulu, for ruining the lady's coat.'

The dog's jaw split into a cheeky, panting grin, and Hazel laughed. 'She's not sorry at all. You need to have a serious word with her. Which reminds me, what are you two doing here? This is private property.'

Ben shrugged. 'We live here. Who're you?'

'You live ... Oh, you must be Jonathan's children. Sorry, I should've introduced myself. I'm Hazel, the new secretary.'

'Hi, Hazel,' they said in unison.

'But I'm confused. I thought you were away at school.'

'It's half-term,' said Ben. 'Two whole weeks off.'

'Yay!' Seth punched his fist in the air.

Lulu barked in sympathy.

'Don't you like it there?'

'S'all right, I suppose,' said Ben.

'We kinda miss home, and Dad,' said Seth.

Hazel smiled reassuringly. 'Well, you're here now, and I expect you'll get to see a lot of him.'

Seth's face clouded over. 'He's always busy.'

'That's because he has to work, dumbo,' said Ben.

'I'm not a dumbo! You are!'

'Am not!'

'Am too!'

'Boys, boys! No need to argue. Of course he's busy, but I'm sure he'll find some time to spend with you over the holidays.'

Two pairs of eyes met Hazel's, and she read the sceptical look in them.

'There's your grandfather too,' she added, having spied George on his lawnmower at the far end of the park.

Seth crossed his arms. 'Grumpy old Grandpa.'

'Maybe he has a reason to be grumpy.' The more Hazel got to know the inhabitants of Combury Manor, the more she realised that all was not well in Paradise; George and Jonathan barely on speaking terms, two children feeling neglected by their father, and a manipulative would-be lady of the manor.

She recalled Jonathan's words: *your time is yours*. She could do nothing about Tabitha and her transparent motives, and so far she hadn't managed to befriend George, but as long as Seth and Ben were home for the holidays, she could try to spend some of her free time with them.

'That leaves us then,' she said cheerfully. 'I don't have to work all the time so maybe we can do something together, now that Lulu has decided she doesn't want to eat me. Your father told me you have a fantastic library. Perhaps you'd like to show it to me?'

The twins greeted her suggestion enthusiastically, and all three headed back to the house, depositing their boots in the scullery which led to the garden. Hazel eyed the stained coat with regret, then hung it on a peg. She'd need to take it to the cleaner's next time she was in town.

The library proved to be an impressive room on the first floor, with a splendid view of the formal gardens and the park at the back. The walls were covered in oak shelving which stretched across the doorway and the window recesses; a spiral cast-iron staircase led to a narrow walkway, where the books at the top could be reached. An ornately-carved fireplace dominated one wall, with an oil painting above it, and in a corner — cosily tucked underneath the walkway — stood a squashy leather sofa.

Lulu made a beeline for the sofa and curled up on it with a doggy sigh.

Hazel studied the portrait above the fireplace. The sitter was a woman, graceful and slender like Tabitha, but with dark hair and dark eyes. Casting a glance at Seth and Ben, she had an idea who the woman was.

'That's our mum,' said Ben, noticing her interest. 'She died when we were little.'

'I'm sorry to hear that. I'm sure you must've loved her very much.'

Seth shrugged. 'We don't remember her.'

'What happened, if you don't mind me asking?'

'She was in a plane crash.' Making exaggerated aeroplane dive-bombing noises, Ben described this as if it was a cool thing to have happened, as only a young boy might do. The action brought a lump to Hazel's throat. How sad for the boys to have lost their mother so tragically. It reminded her of her own loss, and her heart went out to Jonathan and his family.

'Good thing you still have your dad and granddad then,' she said gently. Noticing Seth's face clouding over again, she changed to a safer subject. 'I really like this library. Do you sit in here a lot? I bet you snuggle up on that sofa for storytime.'

'We don't have storytime,' said Ben.

Seth nodded. 'Dad doesn't read to us. We always read by ourselves.'

'Oh, well, would you like me to read to you sometime? It's a fun way of sharing a story.' Hazel felt an unexpected prickling between her shoulder blades. Was it really so hard for Jonathan to find half an hour to spend with his children? It wasn't right. 'How about it? Or are you too old for stuff like that?'

The boys nodded uncertainly.

'That might be cool,' Seth said.

'What kind of stories are you into?'

Ben stuck his hands in his pockets. 'Dunno.'

'Adventure stories,' said Seth.

'Adventure stories. Right, let's have a look.' Hazel ran her hands over the spines and discovered that the books were in alphabetical order by author, which made things a lot easier. Reaching 'S', she stopped and pulled out *Kidnapped* by Robert Louis Stevenson. 'Here's one.'

'When are you going to read to us? Will it be when we're in our beds?' Ben sounded confused. 'That's, like, for babies, right?'

The idea of reading to these two enchanting boys while they were fresh from their showers and in pyjamas was very appealing, but Hazel suspected that to do that she'd probably need a nanny certificate or a CRB check, which she didn't have. Besides, Ben was right, that seemed too childish. Instead, chasing Lulu off the sofa, she sat down and patted the seat next to her.

'Why don't we read some of it now, then maybe we can play something else later? Maybe football.'

'Girls don't play football,' Seth announced as he dropped down beside her.

'This one does, but first we'll read, okay?'

* * *

They read for over an hour, then had lunch with George in the kitchen. In the afternoon they played football in the park where Hazel proved, with a spectacular save in their makeshift goal, that she wasn't 'just a girl'. When they high-fived after their game, she realised that she'd risen a few notches in the twins' estimation, which for some peculiar reason made her feel absurdly pleased.

Just as they were walking back to the house, Jonathan appeared, and the boys ran to his side, speaking excitedly at the same time. His eyebrows rose in surprise when he noticed Hazel coming up behind them.

'I didn't know you'd met my boys, but they seem to have had a good time. I'm glad,' he added, but there was a rueful look in his eyes as if he felt guilty for not having spent time with them himself. To the boys he said, 'Fancy going to McDonald's for tea?'

The boys greeted his suggestion like a pair of excited puppies.

With an arm around each boy, Jonathan's eyes met Hazel's, and she read the uncertainty in them. 'Would you be interested? I know it's nothing fancy, but . . . '

'I'd love to come.'

'Excellent,' said Jonathan, smiling broadly.

Shifting allegiance, the boys grabbed Hazel by the arms and almost dragged her through the house to the waiting Land Rover.

⋆ ⋆ ⋆

At McDonald's, Hazel couldn't help admiring the way Jonathan handled his two lively children. When they announced that they wanted everything on the menu, he explained patiently that fast food wasn't the healthiest thing in the world and only a special treat because it was the weekend. Later, when they squabbled over who was to sit next to Hazel, he was firm but fair and got them to take turns, between their burger and their ice cream.

When they'd had their fill and ran off

to the outdoor playground, Jonathan slumped in his seat. 'Having kids is hard work,' he groaned.

'They're lovely, though.'

Jonathan was watching Seth and Ben through the window with a faraway look in his eyes. 'I only wish . . . '

'What?' Hazel prodded gently.

'I wish they had a mother. It's very difficult being both Mummy and Daddy at the same time. There's no one to share the burden with, or even the good times.' His eyes returned to hers. 'It hurts. I can't describe it any other way.'

Hazel's stomach twisted itself in knots at his words, and she just stopped herself from reaching across the table to take his hand. He was her boss, and she needed to keep her distance. Instead, she said, 'I think you're doing a good job.'

'You do?'

'I do.'

He sent her a brilliant smile, and she smiled back shyly. As they sat grinning at each other, the boys came haring back, complaining about another child who was bothering them, and Jonathan announced that it was time to go anyway. In their agitation, Seth and Ben seemed to have forgotten all about Hazel's presence, concentrating instead on their father. Although there was no reason why this should bother her, she couldn't help feeling a little left out.

★　★　★

The feeling of being an outsider returned later when she went to fetch her red raincoat to bag it up for the dry cleaner's. Instead of hanging on the peg where she'd left it, it was lying on the floor in a crumpled heap, and there were shoe prints all over it as though someone had deliberately trodden on it.

Her immediate thought was Tabitha, but she hadn't been at work today, as far as Hazel knew.

Then there was George, which made more sense. She still hadn't managed to approach him, but she was even more determined now. If he thought he could chase Hazel Dobson away like that, he was in for a surprise.

She'd smother him with kindness, that's what she'd do.

5

It was bright and sunny the next morning when Hazel caught the bus into town to see Aunt Rose. True to her word, Alison stopped outside the manor on her route, and Hazel sat right behind the driver's seat so they could chat.

'I don't mind working on Sundays,' Alison explained. 'Because it's the weekend, people are always in a happy mood. No one bats an eyelid if I make an unscheduled stop or help one of the elderly folk off the bus, because no one's in a hurry to get anywhere.'

In town, Hazel found a dry cleaner open on a Sunday, handed in her red raincoat, and then made her way to Hillview Care Home where Aunt Rose lived. She'd never been there before, although she'd seen the brochures her aunt had sent, and her lips curved with amusement. Hillview wasn't placed on a hill at all, but snugly tucked away on a quiet side road, among 1930s semi-detached houses.

Despite the misleading name, the atmosphere was warm and welcoming, and Hazel was relieved that her great-aunt had chosen so well.

A carer showed Hazel into the residents' lounge. Tastefully decorated in understated pastels and furnished with oak tables and armchairs, it appeared to be both comfortable and practical for people who were elderly or infirm, or both, like Aunt Rose.

Her aunt had dozed off in her wheelchair, and the carer gently placed a hand on the old lady's shoulder. 'Your niece is here to see you, Mrs Dobson.'

The old lady woke with a start, disorientated for a moment. When she saw Hazel, her face lit up. 'Hazel, my dear, you came.'

Hazel bent low to kiss her aunt on her papery cheek. 'I've been longing to see you in your new place.'

'Would you and your niece like some tea?' asked the carer.

The old lady smiled. 'Aren't you a sweetheart? That'll be lovely, thank you.'

Watching the carer disappear, Hazel sat down in a chair next to her aunt. 'I see you've already twisted everyone around your little finger,' she commented, with a wry grin.

'Naturally.' Aunt Rose chuckled. 'And how is this new job?'

Thinking of Jonathan, Hazel smiled shyly, then she remembered Tabitha's beautiful, calculating face, and her smile dropped. 'It's quite different, but I expect I'll get used to it.'

'That bad, eh?' Aunt Rose sent her a sharp look. 'I took the liberty of making enquiries when I heard where you were going to work. Remember my friend, Esther? Her son, Tom, works at the council, and he tells me that things aren't what they appear to be at that place.'

'In what way?' Hazel recalled the strange light and wondered if that was what Esther's son meant.

'There was some building work going on, that's how Esther's boy knew about it. Then they applied for machinery licences, and waste disposal certificates, and what not. And there's all manner of comings and goings in the night, Tom says. It's very mysterious.'

'Jonathan lets some of the outbuildings out to smaller companies,' said Hazel. 'Surely if they've been given permission to do what they're doing, then it's okay?'

Aunt Rose pursed her lips. 'Tom reckons that permission was only granted because of pressure from above.'

'From above?'

'The corridors of power,' Aunt Rose added, in a low voice. 'The government.'

Hazel stared at her great-aunt, momentarily wondering if perhaps the old lady was losing her marbles, then she dismissed the thought. Aunt Rose was as sharp as a tack.

'This is all to do with Gough Associates?'

Aunt Rose nodded. 'And then that woman turns up, the one that looks like a model.'

'Tabitha Fanshawe.'

'That's the name. Anyway, Esther's boy — he has an eye for the ladies — well, he finds it strange that a woman looking like that, with her credentials, etcetera, takes a job so out of the way. She'd want the bright lights of London, that one, wouldn't she? Not rural Norfolk.'

Aunt Rose paused as the carer returned with a tray. When the woman left, Hazel noticed their tea was served in proper china cups.

'You have them well trained here,' she commented, and her aunt grinned back.

'Did you expect I wouldn't? No need to lower my standards just because I'm stuck here now. Anyway, to get back to that woman.' Aunt Rose was clearly warming to her subject. 'So, Tom looks into her background and discovers that she used to work for a large, well-known oil company.' Aunt Rose put her hand on Hazel's arm. 'Don't you think that's strange? Why would an architect work for an oil company?'

Hazel shrugged. 'Beats me.'

'There's more. Gough Associates are working on a contract which involves planning permission from Tom's department. Obviously he's seen their company brochure where all the individual architects' profiles are listed. You know the sort of thing.'

Having tidied away a whole box of these brochures, Hazel nodded.

'There's no mention of the oil company under this Fanshawe woman's profile. Almost as if they're ashamed of it.'

Or hiding something, thought Hazel. But why?

★ ★ ★

They drank their tea then Hazel suggested a tour of the pretty garden behind the nursing home. As she pushed the wheelchair, Aunt Rose talked about the staff and some of her fellow residents, as if she sensed that Hazel needed time to digest this new information about her workplace.

She wasn't sure how she felt about it. The oil industry was big business, and she couldn't see what it had to do with a small firm of architects. And why would Jonathan keep quiet about the connection? Or was it Tabitha herself who'd kept quiet?

Either way, it was food for thought.

★   ★   ★

She left her aunt with the promise that she'd visit again next weekend, and caught the bus back to the manor, contemplating someone else she needed to drop in on that afternoon.

In the kitchen she found cold meats, cheese, a loaf of Irene's delicious home-made bread, and some bottles of soda water and the dark stout she'd seen George drink sometimes, then assembled a picnic in an old hamper from the laundry room.

She found George where she'd hoped he'd be, in the formal garden, cutting back the rose bushes. Spotting her, he scowled.

'What are you doing here?'

'Bringing you lunch.'

'Lunch? Pah!' He turned away and viciously snipped off a twig with his secateurs.

'Aren't you hungry? I'm willing to bet you haven't had anything since breakfast, and it's now two o'clock. Come on, have a sandwich.'

Still with his back to her, George didn't speak for a long moment. 'Sandwiches, eh?' he said at last. 'With proper butter? Not that fancy margarine nonsense which is supposed to be good for your heart?'

'Butter? Oh, lashings of it!'

Hazel thought she caught a glimmer

of a smile. 'You're not on a diet, then? Women are always on a diet.'

'Some of us are quite happy with the size we are.' She sent him a wry smile. 'Although, I wouldn't mind being taller. I had to stand on a chair *and* a box to get this hamper down from the top shelf. Could've broken my neck.'

This time she was sure his grimace counted for smile. 'You'd risk your neck for a grumpy old man like me?'

'No,' she said firmly, as if she was addressing a recalcitrant child. 'I'd risk my neck for a delicious picnic. If anyone wanted to join me, it'd be a bonus. Depending on their level of grumpiness.'

Suddenly he laughed, and the transformation was magical. Gone was the old grouch, and in place was a jovial, elderly gentleman. '*Touché,*' he said, and put the secateurs down in a wheelbarrow. 'We can sit over there.'

Indicating a stone seat against the brick wall at the end of the garden, he offered to take the hamper. Hazel accepted gratefully because it was rather heavy, and followed him.

'I'm sorry about your coat,' he said.

'So it *was* you?'

'You'd guessed?' He nodded to himself. 'Irene said you were smart. Yes, I was coming through the door with firewood, and I knocked it down and nearly got entangled in it. Then I got annoyed, and, well . . . ' He shrugged. 'Is that why you brought me lunch, to butter me up, so I can see what a nice, sensible girl you are and leave your things alone?'

'Is it working?'

Putting down the hamper, George gave her a wry smile. 'Yes, it's working. You'll do.'

The stone seat had been warmed by the sun, and Hazel spread out the contents of the hamper on a tea towel between them. She had no illusions that she and George were now best friends, but he answered her questions about his work on the estate readily enough, even if he was still a little guarded.

'I understand you own a share of it yourself.'

'Only a small part,' he replied, wiping his mouth on a paper napkin. 'Jonathan has the lion's share.'

'Not the bank, then?'

George chuckled. 'My son's far too modest. He's wealthy enough, but he keeps his cards close to his chest. Probably to stop that catty woman from sinking her claws into him.'

Tabitha, thought Hazel. Funny how her name kept cropping up.

'Can't say I blame him,' George continued, 'after what happened with his wife.'

'His wife? Oh, yes, so sad her dying so young, isn't it? Your grandsons told me about it. She looks lovely in that portrait in the library. He must've loved her very much.'

'Tragic, it was.' George sipped his stout from the plastic cup Hazel had brought. 'Although, between you and me, it wasn't a happy marriage. They were going in different directions from the moment they met, I think. Arabella wanted the high-flying career and the bright lights of the city, Jonathan just wanted to be a family man and run a business. Polar opposites. Upset him that they couldn't work it out between them, and when she died, he blamed himself, although obviously he had nothing to do with it. He never says anything, though.' George cast her a sideways glance. 'We don't talk much, as you might've noticed. Which is probably my fault. I said some things about Arabella I shouldn't have.'

'I'm sorry to hear that.' Hazel had briefly glimpsed that side to Jonathan; that little lost boy look. The widower who carried on bravely, trying to be a good father while worrying that he was failing, burying himself in work in the hope that the guilt would go away.

She almost felt sorry for Tabitha and her attempts at ensnaring Jonathan. If she was a career woman like Jonathan's dead wife, Arabella, it seemed unlikely she'd succeed.

'I'm the one who should be sorry. I shouldn't discuss my son with you like this. You just have this way about you . . . '

'Let's change the subject, then.' Hazel recalled what Aunt Rose had said about strange goings-on at Combury Manor. Deciding to plunge right in, she pointed to the east of the park. 'I've noticed a strange, green light at night, coming from that direction. Do you know what that could be?'

George sent her a startled look, then he frowned. 'I don't know anything about a green light. The only thing at the end of the park on that side is an outbuilding where we keep our, uhm, machinery and such. You'd best stay out of there. That stuff is dangerous, and expensive too.'

'Of course, I wasn't pl — '

'Ah, there's Jonathan,' said George. Was it Hazel's imagination, or did he seem relieved? Which was strange, given the fact that he and Jonathan were barely on speaking terms.

Jonathan was walking down the gravelled path with Seth and Ben in tow. Ben was carrying a large, flat parcel.

'We saw you from the library,' Seth called.

'We were just about to tuck into our pizza, but then the boys wanted to sit out here instead,' Jonathan explained.

Hazel's eyebrows rose. 'Pizza? In the library?'

'Awful, aren't I? Feeding my kids junk food in a nineteenth century library. If Mrs Whitmore finds out, I'm for the high jump.'

Running his fingers through his hair, Jonathan smiled. Hazel felt that familiar tug in her abdomen, followed by a feeling of guilt that she could ever have suspected him of any kind of wrong-doing. Whatever went on here at the manor, if anything at all, she was sure he had nothing to do with it.

'Fancy some pizza, Granddad?' Ben held out the box, but behind his apparent high spirits his eyes were wary.

'I've just had . . . ' George began, then looking from Hazel to Jonathan and back to Hazel again, he summoned up a smile. 'Is it pepperoni?'

'Course,' said Ben.

'Then I'd love a slice.'

Ben turned to Hazel. 'You like pepperoni?'

'My favourite, although I quite like cheese and tomato as well.'

'Did you hear that, Dad? Next time we'll order two, and then we can have a real family dinner.'

Ben passed the box to Seth and the boys tucked into their pizzas with gusto. Hazel met Jonathan's eyes over their tousled heads. There was that smile again, and that funny feeling in her stomach. It made her go completely weak at the knees, and it was just as well she was sitting down because she wasn't sure her legs would have been able to carry her.

Family dinner.

It sounded so nice. Having little family of her own, Hazel realised how much she missed it. And the idea of a life with Jonathan, George, and the boys, was suddenly so appealing that she had trouble swallowing.

I'm falling for him, she realised. *Big time*.

6

She left them soon after, returning the hamper and washing up the plates and cups, not wanting to give Irene extra work.

Then she retired to her flat to read a book on Jacobean architecture, which Jonathan had lent her. Normally the subject fascinated her and could keep her enthralled for hours, but after half an hour she had to give up. Instead, she pottered about aimlessly, unable to get the picture of Jonathan and his family out of her mind. In the end, she made herself a plate of pasta for supper and went to bed early.

At least Monday would bring a welcome distraction in the form of her job and finding ways of slipping under Tabitha's radar.

She woke in the middle of the night with a peculiar feeling that everything was somehow too quiet. Her alarm clock showed two in the morning. Groaning, she turned over and tried to go back to sleep, but there was too much on her mind, and she pushed the covers irritably aside.

When she spied the light at the bottom of the park once again, all thoughts of sleep left her.

George claimed to know nothing about the green light, but having seen it several times now, Hazel knew it couldn't be her imagination. Expensive machinery was stored in that outbuilding. What if someone was trying to break in?

Without any thought to the consequences, she quickly put on a tracksuit and a pair of trainers, found her way through the darkened, labyrinthine house, and out through the rose garden. She took no torch with her and had no intention of calling out 'who's there?' as silly women always did in films. She intended to assess what was going on first before alerting anyone else.

Besides, the thought of going into Jonathan's bedroom to shake him awake was enough to send her pulse racing. She imagined him lying tousle-haired among the sheets, his skin warm from sleep, a strong arm stretched out in front of him, cradling a pillow. An impossible heat rose in her face, and she blinked hard to dispel the image.

* * *

She found the outbuilding and was surprised by the level of security around it. Cordoned off by a razor wire fence, the building had CCTV cameras on every corner, as far as Hazel could see, as well as a keypad entry system on the fence gate.

Despite this, the gate stood open. After a moment's hesitation, Hazel stepped through it, conscious of the camera right above the door which thankfully seemed to be angled away from her. The green light from the windows reflected eerily against the shiny leaves of the mature rhododendron bushes surrounding the building, but the windows were too high for Hazel to look through, and she glanced around for something to stand on. Finding a rickety crate, she climbed up, only to be disappointed. The glass was opaque and, although she could see movement inside and hear voices — male voices — she could discern nothing else.

Pressing her ear to the window, she hoped to catch something of what was being said, but the twisting movement, combined with her weight, was more than the old crate could take. Her foot went through the rotten wood with a loud crack, sending shooting pains up her shin.

Her heart jumped into her throat as the door was flung open, and she came face-to-face with one of the men in the shed. That the person was Jonathan should have made her feel relieved, but it didn't. His expression was thunderous.

'What are you doing here?'

'I, er . . . ' Struggling to get her foot out of the broken crate, Hazel tumbled backwards and landed unceremoniously on her behind. Jonathan made no move to help her up, and the deliberate omission almost made tears well up in her eyes. This wasn't the Jonathan she knew.

'I saw the light,' she explained in a small voice, when she got back on her feet. 'George told me you keep expensive machines in here. I thought it was a burglar.'

'And you thought you'd deal with this burglar on your own, did you?' Jonathan's expression was unreadable. 'All eight stone of you?'

Hazel felt her cheeks heat up. 'Hm, put like that, it does sound crazy.'

Jonathan's lips were twitching, but he didn't comment on that. Instead, he said, 'What did you see?'

'See?'

'In the shed.'

'I . . . nothing. I couldn't see

anything through the glass.'

He nodded. 'You have no business here, Hazel, even if you did suspect a burglary. Go back to bed.' With that, he returned to the shed, sliding home a bolt on the inside.

Needing no further encouragement, Hazel ran back to the house, or rather stumbled because of her injured shin. When she got back to her flat, she threw herself on the bed and buried her face in a pillow, utterly mortified.

What must he think of me?

Forget the way their eyes often met, or the way her heart beat faster just thinking of him. Forget the notion that he might be warming to her, as she was to him. He'd seen her at her worst. A busybody, a meddler, someone who poked her nose into things which were none of her business. A Nosy Parker.

How could I have been so stupid?

As she lay with her face in the pillow to hide the embarrassment which still made her cringe, she felt her confidence and credibility evaporate. Perhaps it was best if she admitted defeat and went back to London.

It was the thought of never seeing Jonathan again which brought her to her senses. She knew she was falling in love with him, but whether he felt the same way about her or not, self-preservation dictated that she held her head high and apologised for her idiotic behaviour, like the mature and sensible individual she believed herself to be. The rest was up to him.

* * *

But that was easier said than done.

Jonathan didn't give her an opportunity to apologise the next day. Whenever she was close enough to mention it, there was always someone else around requiring his attention, and when she finally had him on her own for a split second, he merely shook his head.

'Forget it,' he said, almost tersely.

She was left feeling even more like a wayward teenager. In the end she tried to put it behind her, but somehow Tabitha sensed something was up and exploited her hesitation.

Why did she have to be so sharp-eyed? Hazel thought, when Tabitha had sent her on another pointless errand for the umpteenth time.

The final straw was when Tabitha hinted that there was an 'understanding' between herself and Jonathan, whatever that was supposed to mean. By then Hazel was ready to scream. She escaped to the kitchen to offload on Irene.

'Don't take any notice of her,' said Irene. 'She's a bit *Upstairs, Downstairs*, that one. Nothing you can do will change it. The best you can do is be who you are and keep minding your own 'Ps' and 'Qs'. Then you'll be above reproach if it comes to blows.'

Having someone as wise as Irene on her side made Hazel feel a little better, and she returned to the office with renewed determination. There was no reason why she should allow Tabitha to chase her out of a perfectly good job.

★   ★   ★

Jonathan sighed as he put the phone down after yet another lengthy and frustrating conversation with his client, Robert Miles. He liked working with the man and was impressed by his vision for regenerating the area, but Miles wanted to be kept informed of every little detail, which was immensely time-consuming. Jonathan had just reassured his client that their planning application was going through as hoped, but he was certain this wasn't the last conversation they'd have today.

Another problem preoccupied him. When he'd caught Hazel looking in through the windows of his father's lab, his first reaction had been anger and suspicion at what she was doing there, followed by genuine admiration for her pluck. Seeing her awkwardness, he'd believed her when she said she suspected a burglary. He'd liked Hazel from the very beginning; he had a feeling she was the kind of person who'd never be capable of lying without betraying it in some way. No, she'd definitely been telling the truth.

So why had he humiliated her? He'd treated her like a naughty child and knew he owed her an apology. Yet she was acting as if she owed *him* an apology. It baffled him, but whenever an opportunity presented itself to bring it up, he couldn't find the words to express what he felt. It seemed easier to just tell her to forget the whole thing.

Except he didn't want to do that himself. He had to clear the air between them somehow, so that they could go back to their former easy footing. The last thing he wanted was for her to feel awkward around him, and he suspected that was exactly what was happening at the moment. Besides, he really liked her, and the idea of her not talking to him upset him more than he cared to admit.

He swore silently to himself. They had to talk about it, and soon.

Frowning, he looked up as his father entered his office and closed the door firmly behind him.

'Dad? What can I do for you?'

'It's that girl,' said George. 'Your new secretary. Hazel. I want to talk about her.'

'What's she done now? I mean, apart from peeping through your windows.'

'Nothing.' George crossed his arms.

'Then what's the problem?'

Through the glass partition, Jonathan glanced across the office to the far end where Hazel was sitting. She was tapping a pencil against her chin — something he'd come to view as her thinking pose — then she quickly scribbled something on a yellow Post-it note and stuck it to the front of a folder. She seemed completely absorbed in what she was doing.

'I don't trust her,' George continued.

Jonathan's eyes flew back to his father. 'Because of last night?'

'That's only part of it. For starters, she wasn't the one we expected, was she?'

'The other secretary had an accident, and the agency sent a replacement,' Jonathan pointed out.

'Yes, but don't you think that was a little convenient? One girl *happens* to break her leg, and the agency *happens* to have another suitable applicant on their books?'

Jonathan smiled wearily. Ever since his father had been swindled out of his share of the research company by his unscrupulous partner, he'd been para-noid. But whenever he broached the subject, as gently as he could, George's temper would flare up and they wouldn't speak for days.

'I'm sure it wasn't so convenient for the girl who broke her leg,' he said, with only a hint of sarcasm.

George wasn't listening. 'What if she's in cahoots with that other woman, that catty blonde?'

'Tabitha,' Jonathan corrected him

automatically. He felt uncomfortable when his father criticised anyone in his employ, even if there was a good reason. He looked at Tabitha, saw her flicking her golden hair, and pouting and posing as if she knew she was being watched. Then he looked across to pixie-haired Hazel again, whose loyalty to him had made her want to tackle, single-handedly, what she thought was a burglar. He remembered the wounded look in her soft brown eyes last night; it had shaken him to see her like that, and even more so that he'd been the cause of her anguish. She was the polar opposite to Tabitha.

'I doubt it,' he said. 'Like chalk and cheese, those two. Besides, Tabitha has never made any secret of her old job with the oil company.'

'Uh-huh.' George raised his eyebrows. 'Ever asked her why she left them?'

'She didn't approve of the way they were doing business. In her shoes, neither would I.'

'And you believed her? What if she's an industrial spy? What if this Hazel person is one too? Apart from the fact that I don't want people around when I conduct dangerous experiments in that building, I'm not having anyone steal my invention. These new bio-friendly fuels are meant to benefit the whole world, not just some unscrupulous company.'

'You haven't succeeded yet, Dad.'

'That's beside the point. And I don't want anyone in there, trampling all my plants either. Then how will I be able to extract any oils from them? You mark my words, someone will be after my invention. How can you be sure it's not either of them?'

'I can't,' Jonathan admitted, 'but if I go around suspecting my employees of lawlessness, imagine the kind of working environment that would create. I'm not sure about Tabitha, but I think Hazel is exactly who she says she is, and she's a genuinely nice and trustworthy person.' He couldn't be wrong about that, could he?

'How do you know?' George insisted.

'Dad,' he sighed. 'I just know.'

'Like you 'just knew' last time?'

Jonathan's face flushed, but before he could reply, George held up his hands.

'Sorry, son, that was below the belt.'

Shaking his head, Jonathan said in a thick voice, 'No, you were right about Arabella. I wasn't enough for her, couldn't live up to her lofty ideals, and that caused her to look elsewhere. Sad, but true.'

'She was a scheming and manipulative . . . ' George began, but stopped when Jonathan glared at him.

'She was the mother of my children, and I want them to have an unsullied image of her, even if they don't remember her.'

George glared back. 'Fair enough. If they were my boys, I'd want to protect them too. The thing is, as you've noticed, they've taken rather a shine to young Hazel there, and if she isn't who she says she is . . . ' He trailed off.

'Fine, I'll keep an eye on her if that makes you feel better, but I really don't think you have anything to worry about.'

'You'd best let me be the judge of that,' George replied gruffly, and left the office looking far from reassured.

Jonathan returned to his work, but couldn't concentrate. He considered himself to be a good judge of character and a tolerant man, but his father's suspicions of Hazel and her possible motives had struck home. What if she really was here under false pretences? In the short time she'd been at Combury Manor, she'd managed to get under his skin, mainly because he'd let her and because she was so easy to like. When she'd been lying sprawled on the ground with her foot in a crate, all he'd wanted to do was to laugh and scoop her up in his arms; she'd looked so funny and cute. Only years of self-control had held him back.

But what if there was a darker

purpose? Had she guessed that he was ready to get close to a woman again, and was exploiting it?

He shook himself mentally, recalling her expression last night when he'd caught her snooping. He couldn't help feeling that if she truly had been up to no good, she'd have acted differently, less guiltily and more inclined to explain herself. Instead, she'd been mortified — he could tell — and shame-faced. She'd make a terrible spy, he thought with a wry smile.

All the same, he intended to keep an eye on her.

How did the saying go? he thought. *Keep your friends close and your enemies even closer.* Yes, that was it.

Resolutely, he reached for his mobile phone and sent a text to Irene's daughter, Alison. If he paid her extra on top of what he paid her for the cleaning, he could ask her to follow Hazel.

★ ★ ★

Hazel managed to get through the week without incident, developing a mechanism for deflecting Tabitha's barbs. She concentrated on her work and spent her spare time with Irene, and occasionally Ellie, who suggested they went to the cinema one evening to see the latest Julia Roberts film. She played in the park with Seth and Ben, although she was careful to stay away from the outbuilding.

She tried to avoid Jonathan outside work, which wasn't always possible. He and the boys would sometimes eat in the kitchen instead of in their private apartment, and although the presence of Seth and Ben made it a noisy affair, the atmosphere at dinner seemed more strained than it had been before. Jonathan's expression was guarded whenever she met his eyes, and there was something else in them which made her feel as if she was under scrutiny.

George had returned to his usual taciturn self, although several times she had caught him studying her intently across the kitchen table when he thought she wasn't looking. Hazel had to acknowledge that she'd failed miserably in her attempt at getting to know him better, and the realisation depressed her.

It was with relief that she took the bus into town to see Aunt Rose again the following Sunday.

7

Aunt Rose was asleep when Hazel got there, and the carer explained that the old lady had had a disturbed night.

'You're welcome to drop back later,' said the woman, 'although she might be too tired for visitors altogether today. I hope that doesn't interfere with your plans.'

'It's fine. I can wander around town for a bit, then come back.'

She went back to the high street, which was busy with Sunday shoppers and those just out for a stroll on a glorious autumn day. Spying a small park in the town centre, she decided that she'd sit on a bench with a take-away coffee and soak up some sun.

When she left the coffee shop with a scorching polystyrene cup in her hands, concentrating hard on not burning herself, she wasn't looking where she was going and tripped over a wonky paving stone.

With an exclamation, she stumbled forward, colliding with a man coming towards her, and the contents of the cup spilled down the front of his grey tailored suit.

At first neither of them spoke, then Hazel brought a hand to her face in horror. 'Oh, gosh, I'm so sorry! Your jacket . . . it's ruined.'

The stranger looked down with some dismay, then back at Hazel. 'I saw the sign for paint-balling, but I didn't think it was happening in the high street.'

'Look, I'm really, really sorry,' Hazel said. 'If there's anything I can do, perhaps pay for your dry cleaning bill or something, I'd be happy to.'

The stranger tugged at his jacket. 'Believe me, the stain is nothing compared to the scorching heat which is working its way down my trousers as we speak.'

'But coffee . . . ' Hazel began, then she laughed suddenly at the toe-curling image of hot coffee running down his trousers. 'I apologise for burning your, eh, innards.'

'No problem.' The stranger grinned and stuck out his hand. 'Lawrence.'

'Hazel.'

His hand was soft and warm, and for the first time Hazel noticed his looks. Lawrence definitely fitted the description of tall, dark and handsome, with thick brown hair, twinkling green eyes, and broad shoulders. Her eyes widened in appreciation.

Norfolk is just teeming with good-looking men, she thought. Coming here was definitely a good idea.

'So,' said Lawrence, as he took the empty polystyrene cup from her and put it in a bin, 'it seems that I've robbed you of your morning coffee. Please let me buy you another.' He indicated the café Hazel had just left.

'Oh no, there's no need.'

'There's every need. Come on.' He held up a shopping bag he was carrying. 'Besides, I'd like to get changed.'

They returned to the café and picked a table by the window. When the waitress appeared with a menu, Lawrence ordered a cappuccino and a Danish pastry and told Hazel to get whatever she fancied, then disappeared into the Gents. He returned shortly after, looking — if possible — even more handsome in jeans and a T-shirt. Hazel found herself openly admiring him. He was drop-dead gorgeous, so who wouldn't?

Immediately she felt disloyal to Jonathan. Attraction to another person wasn't all about looks, was it? Jonathan had an effect on her which could make her go weak at the knees, and that wasn't something she'd ever experienced before. At the same time, he'd never given her any indication that her feelings for him were reciprocated. And, if Tabitha really did have a claim on him, Hazel was the one who would end up getting burned.

Maintaining a distance between herself and Jonathan was the best option, however upsetting, and perhaps spending time with another handsome man would help.

'Normally I hate going clothes shopping,' Lawrence said, when he sat down, 'but luckily I'd done some today.' Then, when he noticed her embarrassment, he added, 'But enough of that. Tell me about yourself and what you're doing in Combury Cross.'

Lawrence was funny and charming and a good listener, and Hazel enjoyed chatting to him. He asked about her great-aunt, expressing concern over the old lady's frailty and nodding sympathetically when she told him of her parents' tragic accident. She told him about her job, her colleagues, and began to wax lyrical about working in such beautiful surroundings, which was a huge bonus she hadn't reckoned with.

'Sounds like a grand old place,' he said. 'I'd love to see it some time. Are parts of it open to the public?'

Hazel shook her head. 'It's used mainly as company premises and as a residence, although I suppose the parts that are let out might well be open.'

'Let out?'

'The owner lets out the old stables and outbuildings to smaller businesses.'

'What sort of businesses?' Lawrence bit into his Danish with a thoughtful expression. 'It's just that I'm looking to rent somewhere myself, for a company start-up.'

'Well, there's a cabinet-maker and a potter, and there's also a printing company, which sells business cards on the internet. What line of business are you in?'

'I run a firm of accountants,' he said. 'Perhaps I could come and have a look? *If* there are any vacancies,' he added.

Hazel hesitated. Jonathan had given her more or less free rein when she took over the admin role at Gough Associates, and that included being in charge of the business rentals. At the same time, she felt that he'd appreciate being informed. 'I'd have to run this by my boss first. I wouldn't want to go behind his back.'

'Absolutely!' Lawrence smiled winningly. 'Although I can't imagine you doing anything underhand.'

Hazel grinned over her coffee cup. 'You've got me all wrong. I'm not above a bit of sneaking, I'll have you know.'

'Might this be a case of 'curiosity killed the cat'?'

'Almost. It was certainly a very embarrassed cat slinking away.' More than embarrassed, she thought. *Mortified, disgraced, crushed. You name it.*

'Will it make me laugh?'

Hazel regarded him for a moment. There was a twinkle in his eye which told her that he had a sense of humour. Perhaps sharing the story and laughing about it together would banish the feelings of shame which still made her cringe inside.

She made up her mind. What harm could it do anyway? Nothing had happened except that she'd made a fool of herself. She told him the story in a few quick sentences, and Lawrence laughed so hard he had to hold his stomach.

'I'd have loved to see that,' he said, wiping tears of laughter from the corners of his eyes. 'You, with your foot stuck in a crate, and your scary boss towering over you and scowling like a pirate.'

Hazel felt the need to defend Jonathan. 'He wasn't that scary. Just . . . annoyed.'

'Maybe not, but it *is* funny, you've got to admit that.'

'I suppose so.'

'If it makes you feel any better, I'd have done the same if I'd seen a mysterious light in the middle of the night.' Lawrence's eyes shone with mirth. 'And did you ever manage to find out just what was going on in that shed?'

Laughter was a wonderful medicine, Hazel decided, as the tension from the last few days left her body and her smile matched his. 'No, that remains a mystery. But there's always tomorrow.'

Grinning, Lawrence rose. 'Listen,

I've got to go, but it was lovely meeting over coffee. At a table, not down my front, I mean.'

'Oh, please don't remind me!' Hazel groaned. 'By the way, my offer to pay for your dry cleaning still stands.'

'I most respectfully decline. I couldn't let a lady pay for my bills.' He winked and handed her his business card. 'When you've had a chance to speak to your boss about a possible rental, let me know, and if the place is already let out, call me anyway.'

'Why?' The inane question flew out of her mouth before she could stop herself, and she felt the colour rise in her cheeks.

'Why? Because I had fun today and I'd like to see you again, if I may. Perhaps one day we can solve your mystery at Combury Manor.'

He gave her a quick kiss on the cheek and then he was gone, taking his laughter and good humour with him. Hazel felt as if the sun had dulled a little.

Then she pulled herself together. She hadn't been terribly confident in herself the last few days, and naturally she was flattered that someone as charming as Lawrence had shown her — boring old Hazel — this much interest. It didn't make her feelings for Jonathan go away, but it had been a welcome distraction.

Perhaps she was being inconsistent, but what could she do? Jonathan was definitely off-limits.

There was one person, however, she didn't have any ambivalent feelings about, and that was Aunt Rose. She had to get back to see if her aunt was awake, but it made sense to collect her coat while she was still in the town centre.

It was a shock when the dry cleaner informed her that someone had already collected it.

'But . . . ' Hazel began, then stopped and realised she'd just asked for a red coat without handing over the ticket stub. 'Wait a minute,' she muttered. She rooted around in her handbag for a few minutes, checking every nook and cranny, but it wasn't there. She turned to the assistant again. 'Did the person collecting it give you the ticket?'

'Of course,' the girl replied, looking concerned now. 'Is something wrong?'

Hazel was beginning to wonder that herself, but if there was, it wasn't the dry cleaner's fault so she just shook her head. 'No, everything's fine. Thank you.'

Deep in thought, she left the shop. What sort of person stole someone else's old clothes? It made no sense.

⋆　⋆　⋆

Jonathan was in his office when Alison reported back to him on Sunday afternoon. From her expression he knew immediately that he shouldn't have asked her to follow Hazel, but after what his father had said, he felt he had no choice. Now he hoped that Alison had nothing particular to tell him.

He was wrong.

His concern deepened when Alison mentioned that Hazel had been drinking coffee with an unknown man in town. She explained how she'd set Hazel down at the usual bus stop and then driven on to meet a colleague who would take over the route for a couple of hours, safe in the knowledge that Hazel would be with her aunt for a while. So she'd been surprised when she spied Hazel through the window of a café when she should have been at the nursing home.

'And they seemed to be on friendly terms, you say?' he asked her, trying very hard to quell the jealous note which crept into his voice.

'Oh, yes, they were getting on like a house on fire. You know, chatting and laughing, like old friends do. He may even be a secret boyfriend, which would explain why she pitched me a tale that she was seeing her aunt, but that's her business, isn't it?'

Jonathan's insides were in turmoil, but he kept his voice steady. 'Have you ever seen him before?'

'No, but then again, I don't know everyone in town. He didn't appear to be local. A bit too slick for Combury Cross, in my opinion, although he could be a weekend visitor or even a second-homer.' She sniffed disparagingly at the latter.

'Well, thanks anyway for doing this.' Jonathan opened a desk drawer. 'How much do I owe you for your time?'

'Nothing. And I'd rather you didn't ask me again. Hazel is my friend. She isn't snooty, even if she's been to college and all. Unlike some people I can think of.' Alison glanced darkly through the glass partition at Tabitha's empty desk. 'I feel like a traitor for spying on her, and I only did it to prove that you couldn't be more wrong about her.'

'Your loyalty does you credit.' Jonathan smiled, but received only an impassive stare in return. 'Just so you know, I did this for my father's sake. For some reason he's got it into his head that she's up to no good. Losing his company took its toll. I hope you understand.'

Alison appeared to soften. 'Of course I do. I'm very fond of the old guy. If checking up on Hazel makes him happy, I'm all for it. Lord knows, George could do with a break.'

As she was about to leave, Jonathan said, 'It's probably best if you don't tell Hazel anything about this. No need to make her feel we don't like her.'

Because we do, he thought. *Very much.*

* * *

The loss of her favourite coat was a blow, but Hazel put it down to bad luck and nothing else. She realised that if she wanted to, she could easily become paranoid about it, but she didn't want to think badly of anyone she knew. It definitely wasn't Lawrence, because her handbag had been by her feet the whole time they were in the café together, and therefore out of his reach.

She came to the conclusion that she must have dropped the ticket at some point, and that someone had stumbled across it, eyeing the opportunity for a new coat. Although it was galling that anyone could be so dishonest, there was nothing she could do about it, and she didn't mention it to Aunt Rose when she returned to the nursing home.

Her great-aunt was tired, and Hazel felt a stab of concern that the old lady was no longer strong. They spent a pleasant hour together talking about nothing in particular and, when the carer came to wheel Aunt Rose into the dining room for tea, Hazel got up to leave.

Aunt Rose put her hand on her arm. 'She's still on the payroll, you know.'

'I beg your pardon? Who's still on the payroll?'

'That girl.'

Hazel frowned, unsure what to make of that. She suspected that Aunt Rose was referring to Tabitha, which puzzled her, because of course Tabitha was still on the payroll at Gough Associates. Why would her aunt need to point this out? She decided not to delve deeper because, if Aunt Rose was showing the first signs of dementia — something Hazel had thought before — she didn't want to say or do anything which would cause her distress. She merely squeezed the old lady's hand.

'Don't worry about it. I'll see you again next weekend. Hope you feel better then.'

'I'm fine, fit as a fiddle,' Aunt Rose assured her. Although Hazel didn't know whether the old lady was referring to her body or her mind, she just smiled and nodded.

'Now, be off with you before you miss your bus!' Aunt Rose chided.

★ ★ ★

Cheered by her aunt's optimism, Hazel plucked up the courage to call Lawrence on Monday. He didn't seem bothered when she explained that over the weekend her boss had arranged for the last business unit to be let. Instead, he invited her out for dinner in town the following evening — an invitation she accepted gladly, if only to get away from the strained atmosphere.

On the day of her date, Hazel finished work in good time then dithered over what to wear. Lawrence was incredibly attractive, and she wanted to look her best. As she stared at herself in the mirror, having tossed one outfit after another aside in frustration, she couldn't help feeling that someone with Tabitha's blonde and leggy looks was a far better match for him.

Sighing, she settled on a skirt with geometric swirls in green, yellow and white — colours that she knew suited her well — with a plain white shirt and a black jacket. She finished off the look with her favourite pearl stud earrings

'You look nice,' said Lawrence, when he picked her up outside the gates to the manor, and gave her a quick peck on the cheek.

'You too,' she replied. That was an understatement. Lawrence looked fantastic in a charcoal grey suit with a Nehru collar and a white V-neck T-shirt, a style which wouldn't have looked out of place in Monte Carlo. His yellow Lotus sports car completed the playboy image.

'Wow!'

Lawrence opened the passenger door for her. 'You like it?'

'It's fabulous!'

'I'm glad to hear it. It's my favourite, you see.'

'Your favourite?' Hazel strapped herself in the seatbelt. 'You've got more than one?'

He shrugged. 'Only a couple.'

'Gosh, I didn't know being an accountant could be so lucrative.'

'I'm involved in a few other things as well.'

'Evidently,' she said drily.

She didn't have time to comment

further as Lawrence pressed the accelerator, and they took off at a break-neck speed. The ride was the thrill of a lifetime. The engine rumbled like a black panther, and Hazel's hair stood on end as Lawrence rounded the corners with a skill worthy of Michael Schumacher.

I could get used to this, she thought, and then felt ashamed of herself. It wasn't like her to be impressed by the trappings of a wealthy lifestyle. And besides, no matter how hard she tried to ignore it, there was something about Lawrence which didn't quite add up.

Unable to put her finger on it, she pushed the thought aside and resolved to enjoy the evening.

It proved to be as entertaining as their previous meeting. Lawrence regaled her with stories of his ex-colleagues and explained to her the trials and tribulations of setting up a small business. Hazel told him that she still hadn't managed to solve the mystery of the outbuilding, and then confided in him how uneasy she felt about her run-in with Jonathan.

Lawrence sent her a concerned look. 'You say you suspected a burglary. Has it occurred to you that something illegal might be happening at the manor itself?'

Hazel thought of Jonathan's baggy sweaters and unruly hair, and the way he interacted with his boys. She shook her head. 'I can't believe Jonathan would be involved in anything illegal. It just doesn't seem like his style.'

'Oh, Hazel, you're such an innocent!' Lawrence laughed, but he had enough sense to change the subject when he saw her irritated frown.

But his comment *had* annoyed her. She liked Lawrence and was dazzled by his good looks, but she still hated being patronised.

Was she really so blind that she couldn't see what was happening right under her own nose? *Well, we'll see about that.*

That was why, later that evening after

Lawrence had driven her home, she sneaked out of the house again, this time armed with a torch and a small stepladder she'd found in the scullery.

8

Halfway through the park, she realised her folly. The fence was secured by a keypad lock, and even with the stepladder she wouldn't be able to scale it without cutting herself to shreds on the razor wire.

For a moment she hesitated, torn between the impossibility of her venture and the need to show Lawrence that she wasn't mistaken about Jonathan. She was sure she couldn't be. Then she stiffened her resolve and carried on.

If I can't get in, that'll be the end of it, she thought.

* * *

As she'd hoped, the shed lay in darkness, but it was also securely locked. Chewing her lip, she decided to walk around the fence to see if there was an area where it would be easier to climb, but was disappointed. She returned to the locked gate and gave it a frustrated yank.

Then it came to her: the 4-digit number she'd seen on Jonathan's blotter what seemed like ages ago now. Could that be the code for the lock, and had Jonathan scribbled it on his desk in order not to forget it? It was worth a try.

Quickly she keyed in the four numbers as she remembered them — one, five, seven, two — and was rewarded when the lock clicked open. Congratulating herself on her cleverness, she slipped through the gate and closed it behind her.

Now she faced an even bigger challenge; how to get inside the building itself. The shed had a padlock of mammoth proportions.

However, that proved to be easier than she'd expected. Someone, probably George, had left a high window open, and Hazel set up the stepladder right underneath. Even with the ladder, it was a scramble getting up to the window and an even greater scramble sliding through it. She landed in an undignified heap on the other side, on what appeared to be a stack of large plastic bags.

Dusting herself down, she switched on her torch and saw that the bags contained nothing more interesting than compost, fertiliser and topsoil. The whole shed was one giant hothouse. The walls were brick-built, but the roof was glass with the sky an inky black above, and everywhere she turned there were plants — some as tall as eight feet, and none of them specimens that she recognised.

Added to that there was a foetid stench in the air, of rotting vegetation perhaps, which surprised her because although the smell in a greenhouse was often strong and earthy, it was usually pleasant too.

What *was* George doing in here? The place was a veritable jungle.

Quietly, Hazel explored the hothouse while lighting the narrow path between the flower beds ahead of her. To the rear of the building there was a high work table with several bottles and flasks connected with a mass of tubes. In one of the bottles a sickly green liquid was bubbling over a Bunsen burner and, just as she realised that this was where the smell originated, she became aware of movement to her right.

Her heart jumped into her throat and she fled the way she'd come, tripping over a root and tumbling headlong into a tall triffid-like plant. She screamed as it enfolded her in pale green leaves, pushing a cluster of fuchsia pink flowers into her face, and she fought to disentangle herself.

'Careful, you'll wreck it.'

A torch shone in her face, and a hand pulled her up, none too gently, and out of the plant's unwelcome embrace.

'This is the second time I've caught you sneaking around.' Jonathan held her wrist in a vice-like grip. 'What exactly are you up to?'

'I, er . . . ' Hazel's mind raced to think up a suitable explanation, but nothing believable sprang to mind. 'I thought the place was on fire. It looked that way from my window.'

Jonathan wasn't mollified. 'Well, clearly it's not, so you can go now. And don't let me catch you here again.'

He let go of her so abruptly she had to grab onto the triffid for support. The leaves rustled ominously, and she drew back with a shriek. 'T-that thing,' she stammered. 'What is it?'

'Why? Did you think it was going to eat you?'

'Well, I . . . ' She tailed off, feeling the colour rise in her cheeks.

Jonathan glared at her for a moment, then he threw his head back and laughed. 'You're priceless! You'll quite happily walk in the middle of the road in the driving rain, or climb inside a hothouse full of flesh-eating plants without any thought. Whatever next?'

'Are they flesh-eating?' Instinctively, Hazel leaned into him for protection.

'No, I'm just winding you up.'

Sulkily she pulled away, wincing as she put the weight down on her left foot. She must have hurt it when she stumbled, but that didn't give him the right to laugh at her. 'I'm glad someone finds this funny.'

'Actually, I don't.' Jonathan turned serious again. 'I still think you owe me an explanation for what you're doing here.'

'Snooping.' She sent him a mutinous look.

'Yes, I got that part. What I don't understand is when someone tells you a place is dangerous, and you're supposed to stay away from it for your own safety, why do you do the opposite?'

'I was curious, and that's the truth.'

He stared into her eyes as if he was trying to make up his mind whether to believe her or not. What he saw must have convinced him, because in the end he nodded.

Relaxing, Hazel added, 'Anyway, telling me not to do something is like a red rag to a bull.'

'I'll have to remember that. But first you need to get out of here before my father finds you and has an apoplexy. Did you hurt yourself when you tripped? Can you walk?'

'Yes, I think s — aww!' A sharp pain shot up through her leg, and she bit her lip to stop herself from crying out further.

'Did you twist your ankle?'

Hazel winced as he bent down and put a cool hand on it. 'I must've done. But don't worry, I can hobble.'

'Not on my watch. Here, hold this.' He shoved his torch at her, then without further ado, lifted her up in his arms as if she weighed nothing and carried her out of the hothouse.

'What are you doing? This is ridiculous! I'm not a child.'

'No, you're not.' His voice sounded deeper somehow and Hazel shivered, but not with fear.

The moon had come out, and when she lifted her face to his, the pithy remark died on her lips at the look in his eyes. Gone was the merriment which had first attracted her to him, nor did they hold that peculiar suspicion she'd experienced from him in the last week or so. In contrast, they were dark and intense, and his arms, although strong and firm, held her very gently as if he feared she would snap in half.

Her breath caught in her throat. She knew she should distance herself from him — a relationship would never work — but it was as if her body couldn't, or wouldn't, cooperate.

Sighing, she dropped her head on his shoulder as he carried her into the house.

* * *

Reality came back with a bang when she noticed that he turned right at the top of the grand staircase instead of left.

'This isn't the way to my apartment.'

'I'm not taking you back there. I want to have a proper look at your ankle, and my first — aid kit happens to be in my private bathroom.'

'Oh.'

The magical moment had gone, and she allowed him to take her to his quarters, where he set her down on a battered, brown leather sofa in his living room. Pulling up a small footstool, he placed her injured foot on it, propped up by a cushion, and then disappeared down a hallway which led to the bathroom and, presumably, his and the boys' bedrooms. While he was gone, Hazel drank in her surroundings.

Jonathan's place consisted of a large L-shaped living room, with windows facing towards the front as well as the east side of the park. The sofa stood in front of a grand fireplace, separated by a Persian rug. One corner of the room was taken up by a dining table and chairs, where the remnants of the boys' tea was still in evidence, and a desk and book shelves occupied another. The desk was strewn with pens, papers, folders, several mugs and, incongruously, a fire station built out of Lego bricks.

The whole place was just so like Jonathan that Hazel couldn't help smiling.

Jonathan returned carrying a first-aid box, a glass of water, and a packet of aspirin.

'Here, this will help with the pain.'

Hazel popped two tablets in her mouth, while Jonathan took off her trainer and sock, and rolled up her trouser leg. Her ankle was swollen to almost twice its size, and she winced as he gently turned her foot this way and that.

'You've definitely twisted your ankle, quite badly by the looks of it, but I don't think anything is broken. I wouldn't be able to do this if you had.' Grinning, he looked up, and Hazel's heart did a little jig. 'I'm going to put some arnica cream on it for the bruising, and then a dressing around it for support. Don't put too much weight on it over the next few days.'

'I can still work, can't I?' Hazel asked. 'You know, answer the phone and stuff.'

'At least take a couple of days to rest. There's nothing urgent on your desk, is there?'

'I don't think so.'

'Good, that settles it.'

'But . . . '

'No 'buts'. A sprained ankle needs rest.'

Leaning back on the sofa, Hazel tried to relax while Jonathan's cool and efficient hands bandaged her foot, but his closeness and gentleness — combined with her own confusion — was making this very hard.

In the end, to cover up her embarrassment, she said, 'You've done this before, haven't you?'

'I'm a dad; I can deal with bumps and bruises, and the like.' He paused in what he was doing and met her eyes. 'What I find difficult about being a parent is knowing whether I'm giving my children enough emotionally. I often feel I'm coming up short there.'

'They miss you when they go away to school.'

'They said that?'

Hazel nodded.

'Maybe I need to look into local schools for them. That way we'd be together more, and they'd have friends in the area.'

'Why did you choose boarding school, if you don't mind me asking?'

'It seemed like a good idea at the time.' Jonathan finished bandaging Hazel's foot and rested it back on the footstool. 'I went to one myself and so did Dad. And Arabella, well, she had very specific ideas about what was expected of people from our social circle.'

He rose and went to the stereo to put on some music. Mellow jazzy tones filled the room, but the bitterness, which had crept into his voice, still hung in the air. Hazel could see that he was struggling with something. Guilt, perhaps.

'Tradition is a fine thing,' she said quietly, 'but you have to do what's right for you and the boys.'

He returned to the sofa and sat down beside her. 'You're right. From now on I shall listen only to my heart. Anyway, how did you get to be so wise?'

'Me? I'm not wise.'

'Yes, you are,' he insisted. He slipped his arm over the back of the sofa, brushing her neck as he did so and sending shivers of longing down her back. He cupped her face with his other hand. 'I've never met anyone like you, Hazel. You're open and full of fun, but there's a thoughtful side to you as well. It's . . .'

Jonathan's face was suddenly very close to hers, and her lips parted in anticipation.

'Yes?' she whispered. She knew now why she hadn't fallen for Lawrence's charm. He could never make her heart beat faster, the way Jonathan did.

'It's beautiful. *You* are beautiful.'

Their lips met. At first Jonathan's mouth was gentle on hers, softly exploring, then he became more insistent. Slipping her arms around his neck, Hazel responded with the same enthusiasm. Her body moulded itself to his, and every fibre of her being called out to him with desire and tenderness.

Could this really be it? Had she found the love she craved and never thought would happen; the family she'd longed for since she'd lost her parents?

She didn't dare hope for it. She had to be realistic. What was happening between them was probably nothing more than a bit of harmless flirting, but it was . . . oh, so wonderful.

Finally they came to their senses, and Hazel eased away. 'We mustn't, you know.'

Jonathan brushed his hand across her cheek. 'You're right again. This is neither the time nor the place. But it's very tempting,' he added, with a mischievous wink.

'Behave yourself.'

Laughing, Jonathan hugged her. Hazel sighed and leaned her head on his shoulder. It felt good, sitting there, simply embracing and thinking of nothing but him. She knew now that she was hopelessly in love with him, but she had no idea what he felt about her. She didn't want her thoughts to go in that direction, but just enjoy the moment while it lasted.

It didn't take long for the bubble to burst.

'Hazel?' Jonathan asked. 'What *were* you doing in my father's lab?'

* * *

Jonathan cursed inwardly when Hazel pulled away with a puzzled frown.

'I was curious. I already told you that.'

'Yes, but you've got to admit that breaking and entering in the middle of the night doesn't look too good, even if it was just curiosity. By the way, how did you get over the fence?'

'You wrote the access code to the keypad on your blotter. Then I climbed in through a window.'

'Did I? That wasn't very clever of me.' He narrowed his eyes. 'If you were so curious, why didn't you just ask?'

'I asked George about the green light which I've seen a few times from my bedroom window. He denied all knowledge about it, and when Lawrence suggested — '

'Lawrence? The guy you were seen with in town?'

'Yes, but how did you know?' Hazel's brown eyes widened.

Jonathan looked at his hands, hoping that she didn't notice his evasiveness. 'Alison saw you.'

'Lawrence is just a friend.'

'An old friend?' Jonathan's stomach suddenly felt tight with jealousy.

She laughed. 'No. We met because I spilt coffee on him. Luckily, he forgave me and invited me out. End of story.

Anyway, we were talking, and something Lawrence said made me worry about what was going on in the outbuilding. After the lights went out this evening, I decided to take another look.'

'And what did you think was going on down there? Something illegal?'

Hazel's colour rose slightly. 'I suppose so.'

'You're not an industrial spy then?'

'An industrial spy? What on earth gave you that idea?'

Jonathan grinned. 'Can't be too careful. Actually, I never thought you were, but my father . . . well, he's wary of people he doesn't know.'

Seeing the lack of artifice in her eyes and recalling their passionate kiss, was enough to convince Jonathan that Hazel was telling the truth. He felt relief wash over him that she wasn't spying on his father, but even more so because she didn't seem interested in this Lawrence character.

'But why would George worry about

spies?' she insisted. 'There's nothing to see in his lab except plants and more plants.'

Jonathan smiled. 'The plants you saw are jatropha plants, a native species of Mexico and Central America, with a very high oil content; about 37%, I think. The oil can be used for fuel in a diesel engine without being refined, a so-called bio-friendly fuel. Sustainable energy. You've heard of that, right?'

'But hasn't that already been done? I'm sure I read that somewhere.'

'The idea isn't new, but Dad is on the brink of discovering a different way of extracting the oil, which is more efficient than previous methods. Once his invention is widely used, it could give a much greater national yield, and cost next to nothing in the long run.'

'I can't imagine the oil companies being too happy about that,' Hazel commented.

'They're not, and they'll do anything to stop him, which is why he installed all that security. He lost his research with the old company and had to start again, and he's terrified that someone will steal his invention before he can register a patent with the Patent Office. He wasn't too pleased with me when I gave Tabitha a job.'

'What's she got to do with it?'

'Tabitha used to work for an oil company.'

* * *

Hazel stared at Jonathan, unable to believe what she'd just heard. Tabitha had worked in the oil industry, George's invention could potentially render the use of fossil fuels obsolete, and now Tabitha was working with Jonathan. It seemed too convenient to be a coincidence.

Could this be what Aunt Rose had meant about Tabitha still being on the payroll? Whose payroll exactly?

But before she could voice her suspicions about Tabitha, they were interrupted as George suddenly appeared in the doorway.

'Ah, there you are, Jonny,' he said, in his usual gruff manner. 'The boys were looking for you, and when they couldn't find you, they came to my apartment. They're not well. I can't be sure, but it looks like measles. You had it as a child.'

He paused and looked at Hazel in a way she couldn't quite decipher. 'They're asking for Miss Dobson.'

9

'Measles?' Cold fear slid down Jonathan's back, and he rose quickly. 'How can they have measles?'

'I don't understand either,' said George. 'I thought they'd had all their jabs, but I've called the doctor anyway. He'll be here soon.'

Jonathan reached the door in a couple of strides, registering out of the corner of his eye that his father helped Hazel up from the sofa. Torn between concern for her and for his children made him stop and turn, but Hazel waved him away.

'George and I will follow in a minute.'

Seth and Ben were lying top and tail on George's sofa, looking hot and feverish, and Seth was crying.

'I don't feel good!' he wailed.

Jonathan rushed towards them,

accompanied by Lulu, who jumped up from the floor where she'd been keeping guard. She watched the boys, concern obvious in her big brown eyes.

'It's okay, girl,' he said, patting the retriever to thank her for her devotion.

'Dad,' Ben called feebly from the sofa, 'where's Hazel? Isn't she coming?'

This made Seth cry even louder, and Jonathan's heart almost broke. 'Don't worry, she'll be here.'

While he felt the boys' foreheads, his father appeared, supporting Hazel as she hobbled into the room.

Excited, the boys sat up, their eyes shiny with fever. 'Hazel! You came.'

'Of course.' She smiled reassuringly at them. 'Not that you needed me when you have Lulu. Seems she's been looking after you, eh?'

The dog glanced at her charges with soulful eyes, then trotted across the room to Hazel's side, tail wagging.

'They're burning up,' Jonathan said, frowning. 'Dad, there's some Calpol in my bathroom cabinet. Could you fetch it for me, please?'

Nodding, George left the room.

Hazel hobbled closer, using Lulu for support. 'What would you like me to do?'

Jonathan sighed. 'I guess all we can do is give them the Calpol and wait for the doctor to arrive. Looks like it's going to be a long night.'

★   ★   ★

Hazel could tell that Jonathan was seriously worried, which was understandable. But there was something else in his eyes too — a hint of jealousy, perhaps, that they'd asked for her and not him? She put a reassuring hand on his shoulder. 'When kids are ill, only mums will do.'

Immediately, colour flooded her cheeks. *Mums. Why did I say that? What was I thinking?*

But Jonathan didn't seem to have noticed her gaffe. Instead, he helped her sit down. Seth flung his arms around her.

'My eyes are hurting,' he cried. 'I want it to go away!'

Hazel stroked his thick brown hair. 'Shh. The doctor will be here in a minute, and he'll give you something to make you feel better.'

Ben snuggled up to her too. 'Will it taste bad?'

'Oh, probably.' Hazel caught Jonathan's horrified expression at her frank reply. 'The worse it tastes, the better it makes us feel. It's the Natural Law of Medicine.'

'Really?' Two pairs of blue eyes sought hers. Seth had stopped crying and sent her a wary smile.

'Yep.'

Just then George returned with the Calpol and a man in tow, whom Hazel assumed was the family's GP. The doctor was middle-aged, with glasses and salt and pepper hair, and he was dressed casually in brown corduroys and an oatmeal-coloured fleece.

'What have we here?' he said cheerfully, as if it was commonplace for him to be disturbed in the middle of the night by a suspected case of measles. 'Let's have a look at you.'

With a quick glance at Hazel's bandaged foot, the doctor pulled up a chair beside the sofa and beckoned for the boys to come closer to the lamp. Hazel saw Seth squeeze his eyes shut at the light, but he didn't complain.

★ ★ ★

'Haven't you got a proper greeting for your doctor?' he asked.

'Hello, Dr Cooper,' said Ben dutifully.

'How are you, Dr Cooper?' aped Seth.

'That's better.' Dr Cooper examined the boys, turning their heads from side to side to reveal brownish-red spots behind their ears, and shining a little torch into their mouths.

Then he patted their heads, and rose

to speak to Jonathan while Seth and Ben climbed back on the sofa with Hazel. 'It's definitely measles. They have all the classic signs: fever, sore eyes, white spots inside the mouth. Keep them away from school and in bed for the duration of the fever. I'll prescribe some eye drops, as well as antibiotics to avoid any secondary infections, and you can give them Calpol or any other paracetamol elixir to get the fever down.'

Raising his eyebrows at Seth and Ben, who seemed livelier already, he got out his prescription pad. 'And keep them entertained. In my experience, boys that age can't sit still for more than five minutes. Staying in bed will be torture unless they have something to do.'

'I still don't understand,' said Jonathan. 'I know my wife didn't believe in the MMR and wanted the vaccines done separately instead of a triple vaccine, but I thought that they'd had the measles jab. If I'd known . . . ' He tailed off.

'There's nothing on their medical records to indicate that they had it, Mr Gough.' Dr Cooper handed Jonathan the prescription. 'Could this have been around the time of your wife's death perhaps?'

'It must've been.' Jonathan looked stricken, and Hazel ached to put her arms around him.

'No need to feel guilty,' said Dr Cooper briskly. 'It was an oversight, I'm sure. Now you must focus on looking after those two scallywags. I know you have a business to run, but it seems to me you have a ready assistant in your pretty fiancée over there.'

'I'm not . . . '

'She's not . . . ' Hazel and Jonathan protested simultaneously.

'Oh, well, that's a shame.' Dr Cooper sent Hazel a warm smile and took his leave, followed by George.

Jonathan turned to the boys. 'Right, you two, you need to get back to bed.'

'I want Grandad to carry *me*,' said Ben.

'No, I want him to carry *me*,' Seth protested.

'Me first!'

'No, me first!'

Hazel knew where this was heading, and although she was pleased that Seth and Ben seemed to have bonded with their grandfather, an argument between the boys was the last thing Jonathan needed right now.

'Shush, the pair of you,' she said sternly. 'Grandad's too tired to be carrying such big boys. You're perfectly capable of walking, so off you trot.'

'Okay,' they grumbled, but got up from George's sofa without further complaint. 'Will you come too?' Ben asked.

Hazel hesitated. She'd love to tuck them up for the night but sensed that Jonathan needed to spend time with the boys on his own. 'No, I'm going to bed now, but I'll see you in the morning. I'll bring something to play with and some books, if you'd like. You heard the doctor; someone needs to make sure you stay in bed.'

'Yay!' The boys high-fived and scuttled off in the direction of Jonathan's apartment.

To stop Hazel putting too much weight on her injured ankle, Jonathan helped her as far as the door to her own apartment. 'Would you really do that for me?'

'It makes sense. I need to rest my foot, the boys are quarantined, so we might as well entertain each other. It'll be a pleasure anyway.'

Holding her close, Jonathan caressed her cheek. 'What have I done to deserve you?'

'I don't know,' she croaked. Their embrace was making it difficult for her to speak, her knees had turned to jelly, and her heart was galloping like a runaway horse. He pressed his lips to hers, and she returned the kiss with all her passion.

When he finally let her go, she was shaking with emotion.

'We'll talk soon,' he murmured against her cheek.

The following day, Hazel went in search of the boys, armed with a selection of board games and books she'd found in the library.

They'd installed themselves in Jonathan's king-sized bed, with Lulu slumbering at the foot end. Hazel was loath to enter Jonathan's private domain, but his bedroom was very impersonal with just the bed, a wardrobe and an armchair, and she soon got over her awkwardness.

The only concession to his personality was a silver-framed photograph of Seth, Ben and George on his bedside table, and a Turner print on the wall. It was practical and, well, manly, and — like the rest of his apartment — clearly without a woman's touch. That made her feel a whole lot better.

The boys' faces lit up when they saw her, and they bombarded her with questions. Lulu eyed them tolerantly. Then, with a yawn, she rolled over on her back, inviting Hazel to scratch her tummy.

'What have you brought?' Seth asked, pulling at her sleeve. 'Got any good games?'

'I hope it's not Monopoly,' Ben groaned.

Hazel dropped her bags on the bed. 'One thing at a time. Let me just sit down first.'

The boys suddenly realised that she was hobbling and wanted to help her, but she ordered them back to bed and pulled up the armchair. Sinking into the chair, she groaned when Lulu decided to lie halfway across her lap.

'Bad dog, Lulu!' Ben shooed the retriever away.

Seth rummaged in a bag.

'Alison brought you some croissants when she heard you were ill,' said Hazel. 'Try not to get crumbs all over . . . oh, too late, I see,' she added, as Seth ripped the paper bag open and began to tuck in. Ben joined him and soon they were munching away, heedless of the mess they were making.

Hazel shrugged and ordered Lulu to lick up the crumbs, then got out a stack of board games and a copy of *Wind in the Willows* she'd brought to read aloud. Shortly after, they were absorbed in playing Ludo, and Hazel was enjoying herself so much she completely forgot the time.

She spent the next few days with the boys. Lawrence called her on her mobile to invite her out, but she explained what had happened and he seemed to accept that she was unavailable. In some ways, Hazel realised, it was fortunate that she couldn't go out. It wouldn't be fair to encourage Lawrence, not with the way she felt about Jonathan. They still hadn't had a chance to talk about what was happening between them, nor had Hazel had an opportunity to raise the issue of Tabitha's potential involvement with the oil company, but it could wait. Seth and Ben were her first priority.

Getting the boys to take their

medicine proved to be a challenge, however.

'It's so gloopy and horrible,' Ben complained.

Seth griped when it was his turn, and Hazel decided to make a game of it to see if that would help. 'Do you know what the pilot did after he took his medicine?'

The boys shook their heads.

'He did a gloop-the-gloop.'

'Aww, that's really lame!' Pulling a face, Seth swallowed his spoonful.

'Well, let's see if you're any better at telling jokes.'

'Okay, you asked for it,' Seth grinned. 'Why did the pony cough?'

'I don't know.'

'Because it was a little hoarse.'

Hazel rolled her eyes. 'Is that the best you can do? That's even lamer!'

The boys exchanged a look, then grabbed her and pinned her down on the bed where they tickled her until tears of laughter sprang into her eyes.

'Stop, stop! You're killing me!'

'I see my patients are improving.' Jonathan was standing in the doorway, eyeing their tussle with a wry grin. 'If I didn't know any better, I'd think you were all guilty of faking it.'

The boys rushed to their father excitedly, while Hazel tried to tidy her dishevelled appearance. Their eyes met over the heads of the twins, and Jonathan's tender expression made her breath catch in her throat.

There's no going back now, she thought. *If you keep looking at me like that, I'll never want to leave.*

★ ★ ★

Her foot improved quickly, soon causing her no more trouble than the odd twinge when she walked on it. On Friday afternoon, George appeared in the sick room with a message that Jonathan was throwing a small party in the office.

'He'd like you to join the celebrations.'

'I'll be right there.' Hazel closed the book she'd been reading to the boys. 'But what about . . . ?'

George gave an impatient wave. 'Don't worry, I can take over from here; I read *Wind in the Willows* to Jonathan many times when he was a boy.'

Seth and Ben were fascinated that their father had once enjoyed the same book, and they let Hazel go without too much protest.

When she arrived, the others were all assembled clutching glasses of champagne. The office was festooned with banners, and in the middle of the room a trestle table had been put up and was groaning under the weight of several platters of food, nibbles and drinks.

Smiling, Jonathan handed Hazel a glass of champagne. 'I'm glad you came, and just in time. I'm about to say a few words.'

Hazel went to stand next to Ellie. 'What are we celebrating?' she whispered.

'The Robert Miles contract,' Ellie

whispered back. 'Planning permission has finally gone through. Jonathan is pleased as punch.'

Having been so busy looking after the boys, Hazel had forgotten about the real world, but she was happy that work had gone according to Jonathan's hopes.

'I see your foot is better,' Ellie commented. 'How did it happen?'

Hazel grimaced, but was relieved that Ellie didn't know exactly what had taken place. 'I tripped in the garden. I've always been a bit clumsy.'

Ellie gave her a quick hug. 'You poor thing.'

Someone shushed them as Jonathan began to speak. He started by thanking everyone for their hard work and dedication, then went on to talk about the progress of the project and what it would mean for the company.

★   ★   ★

Jonathan's eyes found Hazel's. 'I'd also like to thank Hazel. Although she hasn't been here long, she's helped us get a very untidy operation in order, and in the last few days we've all felt her absence keenly.'

There were murmurs of agreement from the others.

'Not only that, but she's shown me what really matters,' Jonathan continued, and raised his glass. 'Here's to our future.'

The toast was directed at everyone assembled, but Jonathan's emphasis on the word 'our', and the way his eyes never left hers, made Hazel think that perhaps he was sending her a special message. She was confused by his attention and didn't know what to make of it, but that didn't stop her cheeks from heating up. Ellie noticed and elbowed her in the ribs.

'Some food might take your mind off it.'

They helped themselves to food, and so did their colleagues. The mood was high, and soon the office was a noisy hubbub. Hazel stood a little to one side with her plate and watched Jonathan move about the room, shaking a hand here and slapping a back there.

Suddenly, he appeared at her side. 'Enjoying yourself?'

'Er . . . oh, yes, very much. It's a lovely party.'

He sent her a concerned look. 'Are you sure? Because I really want you to.'

'Thank you, yes. I was just thinking about Seth and Ben.'

'I'm sure my father can cope. He'll have to, because I'm going away tonight. Robert Miles is starting another project in Lincolnshire and has asked me to visit the site with him, but I'm back Saturday afternoon. I'll leave you my mobile number just in case.'

'We'll be fine,' Hazel reassured him. 'I'll try not to leave it all to George.'

'I know you won't.' Jonathan stroked her cheek briefly. The touch was feather-light, but made her entire body tingle. 'And when I get back,' he added in a low voice, 'there's something important we need to talk about.'

He pressed a quick kiss to her lips then turned away when one of their colleagues demanded his attention. While Hazel was still reeling from the impact and the significance of him kissing her in such a public place, her eyes met Tabitha's across the room.

There was no disguising the venom in those baby blues. It was a look of pure hatred.

10

Jonathan said goodbye to his children when he left in the early evening, with strict instructions that they had to behave themselves. While their grandfather gave them their tea and made sure they had a shower, Hazel helped Irene tidy up after the party, then she went to tuck in the boys.

'Please stay,' they begged. 'There's this really good bit in the story, but Grandad's too tired to read any more.'

'If it's okay with you, I'd like to turn in now,' George admitted.

Hazel noticed he looked weary, slightly stooped and with dark circles under his eyes, but it was no surprise since he often worked in the lab late into the night. 'I'd be happy to.'

George said goodnight in his usual gruff manner, but Hazel sensed that his relationship with his grandchildren was improving, and that pleased her. With no mother in their lives, having a close bond with their grandfather was doubly important.

'Can you sit between us and read?' Ben asked. 'That's what Grandad does.'

The boys patted the space between them expectantly, and Hazel vacated the armchair in favour of the bed, grabbing a blanket to put over her legs while the twins snuggled down in their duvets.

She read for about an hour until they fell asleep. Yawning, she debated with herself whether leaving would wake them, then she decided to stay a while to make sure they'd dropped off completely.

It was cosy and warm between the boys, and it wasn't long before Hazel's head fell back against the headboard, and sleep overtook her.

★　★　★

175

She was shaken awake by an agitated George. It was early morning, and a pale autumn sun was streaming in through the window where she'd forgotten to draw the curtains.

Making sure the boys were still sound asleep, she sat up groggily. 'Sorry,' she whispered. 'I didn't mean to fall asleep in here.'

'Never mind about that. My lab has been burgled.'

'Burgled?' Hazel slipped out of bed quietly and smoothed down her crumpled clothes. 'Have you called the police?'

'They'll be here in an hour. I've called Irene as well, although she doesn't normally come in on Saturdays, but with Jonathan away . . . Well, Irene is a rock.'

Was it her imagination, or was George's interest in the housekeeper more than just professional? Interesting, she thought, and couldn't help welcoming the idea.

In the kitchen, Irene was preparing a fried breakfast.

'What a to-do,' she said, although she looked her usual unruffled self. 'I thought we could do with a big breakfast before the police get here. George, stop pacing and sit down. There's nothing anyone can do till then.'

Only then did Hazel notice how haggard George looked. He'd been tired the night before, but it was nothing compared to this hollow-eyed spectre. It was as if he'd aged ten years overnight.

Her heart went out to him. He'd suffered a terrible setback once, and now it seemed as if it had happened again. Not only had his property been violated, there was all his research to consider. How much had he lost this time?

Reaching across the kitchen table, she put her hand on his arm. 'I'm sure everything will be all right.'

Unconvinced, George gave a curt nod.

Irene forced them to eat breakfast,

although they both struggled. When a police constable arrived, the housekeeper had coffee ready.

The officer, a fresh-faced rookie, took down the details then went with George to have a look at the lab. Hazel organised breakfast for Seth and Ben and, judging them to be sufficiently recuperated, told them to get dressed. By the time she'd finished, the constable was ready to leave.

'Call us when you've looked through the CCTV footage,' he said to George. 'You might recognise your burglar, or at least it'll give you an idea how they got in through the main gate as well as inside the lab. I'll send a chap around later to check for fingerprints, so no one should disturb the crime scene in the meantime.'

'I'll wait for Jonathan to get back,' said George, when the policeman had left. 'I don't really understand all this newfangled nonsense.'

Hazel watched him leave the kitchen. More than ever, Jonathan's father looked like a broken man, and she was tempted to run after him and hug him until he felt better. But she knew he'd hate that.

★   ★   ★

When Jonathan arrived back in the afternoon and saw the police car parked in front of the house, his first thought was that something had happened to the twins. He almost flung himself out of the Land Rover and raced upstairs.

Finding his apartment empty, he headed for the kitchen, having noticed Mrs Whitmore's Nissan in the drive. To his relief, the boys threw themselves at him, babbling over each other and making no sense at all.

Hugging them close, he said, 'Whoa, one at a time! What happened?'

'Grandad's shed's been burgled,' Seth explained, his eyes shining as if this was the most exciting thing in the world.

'Really?'

'I'm afraid so,' said George. 'I called the police. There's a technician down there now, checking for fingerprints.'

Jonathan's eyes fell on Hazel, who shrugged, and Mrs Whitmore shook her head imperceptibly. Clearly no one knew any more than that.

'Any idea who did it? Have you checked the cameras?'

George shook his head.

'Well, we'd better go and do that now,' Jonathan said, taking charge. 'We need to see if there's anything which might help the police catch the culprits. Mrs Whitmore, any chance you could make some coffee, please? I've had a long journey.'

'I'll do it so Irene can get home,' said Hazel. 'It's been a hectic day.'

'Thanks. We'll be in my office.'

He touched her lightly on the arm and was gratified by her heightened colour. During his time away, he'd come to realise how much he cared for Hazel. By telling her how he felt, he risked exposing himself, but he had to do it. Otherwise, how would he ever know what might be between them?

But first he had to deal with this burglary.

In the office, Jonathan fired up his computer and logged into the hard disk containing the footage from the various security cameras. 'I doubt if your burglar climbed over the wall, so let's check the camera on the main gate first.'

They trawled through hours of footage, and although they were able to play it back faster than normal speed, it was a tedious task. Hazel brought the promised coffee on a tray, with the boys carrying a mug each, then they retreated quickly and left them to it.

He hadn't had much sleep the night before on the uncomfortable hotel bed, and although the coffee helped, Jonathan felt his eyelids grow heavy.

Suddenly George grabbed his shoulder. 'There! Stop! Back up a bit. That's it.'

An incriminating scene played out in

front of them. A man with a bolt cutter appeared outside the locked gate, signalling to someone on the inside, who then came into view of the camera. It was a woman, dressed in a trench coat, jeans, and with a scarf tied around her head. Taking out a bundle of keys, she unlocked the wrought iron gates, keeping her face turned away from the camera as if she was familiar with its location. The man slipped through the gate, the woman locked it again, and they both disappeared from view.

'Well, I'll be . . . that's Lawrence!' George exploded, clenching his fists. 'The scheming toad!'

'Lawrence?' An icy feeling slid down Jonathan's back, and it was as if his own voice came from far away. He'd heard that name before. Hazel's friend. The one she claimed to have only just met.

'The son of my old business partner,' George explained. 'His father wasn't able to carry on with my research without my notes, but he knows my invention is worth a lot of money if they can sell it to one of the oil companies. Money is all they ever cared about,' he added with a contemptuous snarl.

'And did they succeed in stealing it?'

'Harrumph. What they took won't make any sense to them. I keep all my important findings up here.' George tapped his head, then focused on the CCTV footage again. 'Who's the woman, I wonder? And how did she get hold of a key?'

'I don't know,' Jonathan replied, but it was a lie. He did know. He'd have recognised that raincoat anywhere, the style and the cut unmistakable even on a black and white security film.

The woman letting in the burglar was Hazel.

* * *

Hazel was tidying up in the kitchen when Jonathan sought her out.

'A word, if you please.'

'Of course.' She dried her hands on a tea towel.

Jonathan got right to the point. 'You let the burglar in. Your friend Lawrence.'

Confused by his words, Hazel blinked. '*Lawrence?* What are you talking about?'

'Don't bother denying it. You were caught on CCTV wearing that red raincoat of yours. I'd recognise it anywhere.'

'My raincoat? Oh, but someone collected it from the dry cleaner's, and — '

Jonathan held up his hand and sent her a look of contempt. 'I don't want to hear it. You've already explained yourself to me too many times. I should've seen through it, but I was blinded by your pretty face.'

'Jonathan, listen, I — '

'I want you to pack your things and leave. Right away. And I don't want to see you ever again.'

He turned on his heel and left. Wringing the tea towel in her hands, she tried to make sense of what he'd said. Lawrence was a burglar. Someone had let him in during the night, wearing Hazel's raincoat as a disguise. Which meant she'd been set up. Meeting Lawrence, losing her dry cleaning ticket, having allowed herself to be goaded into breaking and entering — it had been a set-up from start to finish.

But who was behind it, other than Lawrence? Tabitha? Maybe, maybe not, but there was no way Hazel could prove it. And Jonathan seemed to have made his mind up about her 'guilt' anyway.

The reality of the situation hit her. Jonathan never wanted to see her again. That meant never seeing Seth and Ben either, nor George and Irene, and everyone else she'd come to like and respect in this wonderful place.

Stifling a cry with her hand, she stumbled towards a chair. It was like losing her family all over again, and she wrapped her arms around herself to quell the horrible, sick feeling that her heart had been ripped out. It was almost too much to bear.

How long she sat on the hard kitchen

chair, she had no idea. Finally she rose, slowly because her legs were shaking, and went to her apartment to pack.

★ ★ ★

Swirling the ice cubes in his drink, Jonathan stared out into the dark. Standing by the large window facing the front drive, he was in exactly the same spot he'd been earlier when he'd watched Hazel struggling down the gravelled path with her bags. The gentlemanly thing would have been to help her to the bus stop, but he'd found himself unable to do that.

The anger was still there, pushing against his ribcage from the inside so hard he feared his chest would explode. Anger at Hazel's betrayal, anger that his father's work had left them all so exposed, but mostly he was angry with himself for being taken in.

I'll never trust another woman for as long as I live, he thought for the umpteenth time.

But behind the anger was the realisation that he'd fallen in love with her, and it was like an open wound which wouldn't heal. The sense that he'd lost something precious before he'd had a chance to hold it, gripped his insides and made even simple acts like lifting a glass to his lips physically painful. Whatever her betrayal, and despite his own righteous anger, he couldn't just make those feelings disappear. It would be a long time before he got over her. If he ever did.

He was startled out of his thoughts by movement behind him. 'Dad?'

'Ben? Why aren't you asleep?'

'Is Hazel going to come and sleep in our bed again tonight?'

Jonathan frowned. 'In your bed?'

Ben shrugged. 'She was reading to us.'

'How do you know she was in the bed with you, if you were asleep?'

Chewing his lips, Ben lowered his eyes. 'I woke up, and it was, like, really late, but I couldn't sleep so I played with my Nintendo for a bit. I was worried the beeping noise would wake her, but it didn't.' He looked up again. 'Are you cross with me? I know I'm not supposed to play Nintendo in the middle of the night.'

Jonathan stared at his son while his mind was working overtime. His heart lifted at the thought that his suspicion of Hazel might be unfounded. Perhaps she hadn't forsaken him after all.

'No, I'm not angry,' he said, and gave Ben a quick hug. 'In fact, I'm very glad you told me. Now, let's get you back to bed.'

He waited until he was sure Ben had fallen asleep again, then rushed to his office and switched on the computer. If Hazel had been asleep between the boys all night, who was the woman in the raincoat?

Calling up the security footage again, he played back the section from the main gate, paying particular attention to the woman. Recalling how perfectly that coat had fitted Hazel when he first met her, it became clear on closer inspection that both the sleeves and the body were far too short for the person wearing it in the picture.

In fact, the height and stature of the mysterious woman was a closer match to Tabitha than Hazel.

He sat back with his eyes frozen on the screen, his stomach churning and his palms sweating. Overcome with despair, he realised that he'd made a terrible mistake.

★ ★ ★

Tabitha wasn't in when he arrived at her flat in Norwich, but he wasn't surprised. Tabitha liked going dancing on Saturday nights, so he settled down in the car to wait for her.

Later, a knock on the Land Rover's window brought him out of his involuntary slumber.

'Cooey! Have you come to see me?'

'Where have you been?' Squinting at

the morning sun, Jonathan stepped out of the car.

Tabitha pouted. 'Clubbing. Is there a problem?'

'I need to talk to you.'

'Well, come on up.'

He followed her up the stairs to her flat, conscious of the questioning glance she sent him over her shoulder.

'I'll get the coffee on,' she said, in her most sultry voice. 'You look like you could do with some.'

'Fine.' He didn't really want coffee but it postponed the moment when he had to confront her. Confront her with what exactly? He had nothing to go on, except a hunch, and he wasn't sure he could trust even his hunches these days.

While Tabitha was in the kitchen, his eyes roamed the décor of her living room — all glass, chrome and white furnishings, which wasn't much to his taste. He slumped down on her pristine sofa, realising only then how tired and confused he felt, and adjusted an expensive-looking silk cushion. Something dug into his back. Pulling the offending article out from under the cushion, he froze.

It was a crumpled red raincoat.

Smiling, Tabitha appeared with coffee on a tray, but her smile dropped when she saw what he was holding, and she put the tray down.

'Would you like to explain yourself?'

She gave a tinkling little laugh. 'How did that get there? I've been looking for it everywhere.'

'It's not even yours.'

'Of course it's mine. Who else would it belong to?'

'There was a break-in at the Manor, the night between Friday and Saturday. Two people were caught on CCTV, and one of them was wearing this coat, which, by the way, is far too small for you. Hazel claimed that someone had collected her coat from the dry cleaner's, but I didn't listen. I should have.'

Realising that the game was up,

Tabitha sank into an armchair with a dramatic sigh. 'I did it all for you, Jon-nee.'

'For *me*?'

'I thought we had something.'

'What gave you that idea? I respected you as a colleague, and I admit you are very attractive,' Jonathan replied, 'but that's all. I've never given you the impression that I had any tender feelings towards you.'

'*She* turned your head,' Tabitha snarled, with a sudden nasty expression on her face. 'I noticed that as soon as she arrived. When my old colleague, Lawrence, contacted me, I saw a way of getting rid of her and helping him at the same time.'

'So you decided to frame Hazel by deliberately stealing her coat?' Jonathan's voice was cold and hard, but she hardly seemed to notice.

Tabitha just shrugged. 'She'd dropped her dry cleaning ticket in the office, and I collected it to annoy her. That it was a coat proved to be useful, but it was mere chance.'

'So how did you get in again after the party? I thought all the gates were secured.'

'I stayed behind afterwards, and took the gate keys from your office. As for the fence around the shed, I'd seen the code for the keypad on your desk, and I knew where the camera was.'

She looked almost proud of herself, while Jonathan had to fight an urge to wipe the smug grin off her face.

'Are you going to have me arrested?' she asked, with a toss of her hair. 'You can't prove anything.'

He noted the challenge in her words, but didn't rise to it. Any admiration he'd had for Tabitha had completely evaporated. 'No, but Lawrence will be. Whether he spills the beans on you or not, is up to him. In the meantime, you can expect the paperwork in the post for dissolving our company partnership. I suggest you sign.'

Clearly she hadn't considered the

possibility that Lawrence might implicate her, and her face paled visibly. Carrying Hazel's raincoat over his arm, Jonathan left Tabitha standing in the middle of the room, struck dumb.

* * *

He called Alison from the Land Rover. 'When you picked up Hazel yesterday, where did you take her?'

'To Sunnyside B&B, just off the high street. Why? Jonathan, what have you done?'

'Only made the biggest mistake in my life,' he replied, and hung up.

Sunnyside was tucked away in a quiet cul-de-sac, and fortunately there was a parking space right outside. However, Hazel wasn't there.

'The young lady checked out early this morning,' explained the proprietor. 'She seemed in a hurry.'

'Do you know where she was heading?'

'The station, I believe. Wanted to catch the — '

Jonathan didn't hear him out. He jumped back in the Land Rover and reversed out into the high street, the vehicle's tyres squealing as it roared off.

Because of his stupidity, Hazel was going to disappear out of his life. He couldn't let that happen. He had to catch her, and if that meant getting a speeding ticket, then so be it. The alternative — never seeing Hazel again — was unthinkable.

★   ★   ★

Hazel watched the young family as they entered the platform. The father was pushing a pram with a baby inside, the mother carrying a weekend bag and with a tight grip on the hand of a little boy. The baby dropped her bottle and the father picked it up, sending his wife an affectionate grin. The ordinary, domestic scene made Hazel swallow hard, and she had to look away to prevent the tears she'd refused to shed during the night.

She didn't blame Jonathan for believing only what his eyes told him. Most people would. She blamed herself for being a fool, for not seeing it coming. For falling in love and making everything so much worse for herself.

Yesterday, when visiting Aunt Rose, she'd blurted it all out, and her aunt had comforted her as best she could. However, there was no cure for a broken heart, they both knew that. Aunt Rose had encouraged her to go away for a while, despite Hazel's protests that she wanted to stay near her. Eventually, she'd come around to the idea.

She'd called her former flatmate in London, who was very sympathetic and had said Hazel could have the box room in the flat for as long as she wanted it, since her old room had already been let out again.

It didn't matter to Hazel that she'd

be sleeping on a camp bed; she just needed to put some distance between herself and Jonathan while she considered her future.

But what future could there be without Jonathan? Or the boys? Her heart contracted at the thought, and she had to swallow again.

'A penny for them.'

★ ★ ★

Jonathan could have kicked himself when Hazel stepped back in alarm, as if she thought he was going to hit her.

'I know you didn't do it,' he said, slightly breathless from his frantic dash through the station building. 'Tabitha stole your raincoat to make it look like you did. Can you forgive me for not believing you?'

She stared at him, her expression inscrutable. Realising that the situation required a different tactic, he surprised even himself by going down on one knee in front of her.

'I love you,' he said. 'Will you marry me?'

'But . . . '

'And you're not allowed to say 'no'. I am, after all, your boss.'

★　★　★

Hazel felt the eyes of other passengers on them, and the colour rose in her cheeks. She wished she didn't have this awful tendency to blush. 'Jonathan, you . . . this is really embarrassing. Please get up.'

'Not until you agree.' Grinning broadly, he rose anyway and placed his hands on her shoulders.

Looking up into his handsome face, Hazel composed herself and a smile stole over her lips as she pointed out something he seemed to have forgotten. 'You sacked me, remember?'

'I'm revoking it.'

'Really? Just like that?'

He drew her close for a gentle kiss. 'Just like that.'

Sighing against his chest, she wanted to remain realistic. 'The thing is, Jonathan, you already have everything: great kids, a loving dad, even if he doesn't show it. A beautiful house. Money. Staff who dote on you. You don't need me.'

Holding her away from him, he said, 'How about this? I love your smile, your sense of humour, your kindness, even the way you get yourself into impossible situations. Your unpredictability brightens up my day, and I don't think I can live without you. Will that do?'

He pulled her into a hot embrace, which raised whispers among the onlookers. Hazel's heart soared, and she felt herself melt into him.

'I don't know. You'd better kiss me again to make sure.'